W9-DCP-964

Antique Shop Mysteries™

The Crate Beyond

Pam De Voe

Annie's®
AnniesFiction.com

Books in the Antique Shop Mysteries series

Library of Congress-in-Publication Data
The Crate Beyond / by Pam De Voe
p. cm.
I. Title
2017947343

AnniesFiction.com
(800) 282-6643
Antique Shop Mysteries™
Series Creator: Shari Lohner
Series Editor: Elizabeth Morrissey
Cover Illustrator: Bonnie Leick

10 11 12 13 14 | Printed in South Korea | 9 8 7 6

1

Maggie Watson pulled her sweatshirt sleeves down over her wrists as she entered her cool, sunlit kitchen. Brilliant beams of early morning sunlight bounced off the coffeepot and toaster. *I hope the rest of the day is this beautiful,* she thought, making her way to the coffee maker.

Once her coffee was brewed, she settled down on a chair at the breakfast table and gazed out the window. Fluffy cumulus clouds slowly wandered by on a pastel-blue backdrop. Hands wrapped around the porcelain coffee mug, elbows on the table, she allowed herself to simply enjoy the moment. She glanced down at the cup as the coffee's warmth spread through her.

The emerald-green university logo on the mug's side showed signs of use, as well it should. Her late husband, Richard, had given her the cup on the afternoon he came home and announced his acceptance as a new professor at the university, where he would be the resident expert on historical archaeology in the Eastern United States. She ran a finger around the logo. That was more than twenty years ago. They had just started their family, and life had been good for more than a decade. But then, Richard had succumbed to an unexpected aortic aneurysm a few years ago, and life had changed forever.

Maggie leaned forward and returned her gaze to the sky. Watching the clouds slowly move, she mulled over the major changes in her life since her husband's death. Their daughter, Emily, had graduated from high school and gone off to Maine to study nursing. In another surprise turn of events, Maggie had moved to Maine as well when her Aunt Evelyn passed away and left her the historic Sedgwick Manor in Somerset Harbor, which came with a business called Carriage House Antiques.

So many changes, both expected and unexpected. Maggie was reminded of one of her father's favorite sayings: "Nothing remains constant except change." *How true.*

Maggie rose and refilled her cup, then headed into the library to check her e-mail. Before she sat down at the desk, she glanced out the window at the road, which was empty except for a small, silver car parked at the curb near the house. She stared at the car for a moment to determine if it belonged to anyone she knew. She shook her head. It wasn't familiar. This was the beginning of tourist season along Maine's coast, so the driver, just barely visible behind the wheel, was likely an out-of-towner.

If the weather was good, there would be many more tourists coming to enjoy the seacoast and the charm of her town. And of course, visiting her antiques shop. Thanks to preparations by her savvy shop manager and good friend, June McGillis, Carriage House Antiques would be ready and able to serve the new waves of customers delighting in their merchandise.

Maggie took her place at the flame mahogany partner's desk and booted up the computer, then opened her e-mail. As she skimmed the new messages, she noticed one with a surprising subject line: *Native American Archaeology Materials Erroneously Sent to You.* Clicking on it, she read:

Dear Mrs. Watson,

I am sorry to inform you that we have discovered a mix-up in the materials sent to you from Dr. Watson's archaeology lab. Student helpers inadvertently included several boxes from field studies of Professor Daniel Faber, who specializes in the

Ancestral Puebloans of the American Southwest. Unfortunately, this error was only discovered recently as the professor was cross-checking earlier research.

Professor Faber or his assistant will be contacting you shortly to recover the boxes.

We apologize for any inconvenience this may have caused you.

Sincerely,

Betsy Hanover, secretary

Department of Archaeology and Anthropology

Maggie stared at the screen. Her hands felt clammy and cold, yet sweaty at the same time. Her breath caught in her throat.

Richard. While he was never far from her mind, seeing his name in the e-mail from the departmental secretary opened a chasm in her heart. He was gone, no longer able to share her life, her daily routines, her joys and sorrows. Touching the bridge of her nose, she bent her head.

In coming to Maine, she had managed to deal with being a widow by jumping fully into her new life of running her aunt's well-known antiques shop and managing the incredible estate. But this e-mail reawakened a long-dormant sense of loss. Her eyes stung and began to fill with tears.

After a moment, she took a deep breath and reread the message. She didn't recognize the secretary's name, so Maggie assumed she was a newer hire. *Change really is constant.*

Maggie hadn't opened any of the boxes Richard's department

had sent to her after his sudden death. At first, she admitted to herself, the task was too emotionally overwhelming. Later, she found it easier not to have to face the pain she had been certain opening each box would bring. Those boxes represented her husband's life's work.

As she covered her eyes with her hand, something warm and soft brushed against her leg—her trusty tabby cat, Snickers. He could always read her feelings and knew when he was needed.

"Come here, you rascal," she said, choking back the raw emotion that had been threatening to take over. She picked him up, set him on her lap, and rubbed his chin. He stared up at her.

"You think I'll be all right, don't you?" she asked him. His intense green eyes never left her face. She stroked his back and reread the secretary's e-mail for the third time.

Maggie sighed. "I guess this means I'll finally have to go through Richard's boxes from the university. He'd never want to delay someone else's research."

She crinkled her nose as she thought of the daunting task ahead. The boxes the secretary mentioned were spread between the Sedgwick Manor attic and the carriage house storage area, separated arbitrarily during her move from Vermont. She'd had no reason to go through them until now. *Out of sight, out of mind,* she mused. *This could take a while.*

After taking a deep breath, she said, "No time like the present, right, Snickers?"

Snickers meowed.

Maggie grinned in spite of herself. "Okay, let's head up to the attic."

As she and Snickers climbed the stairs, Maggie formed a plan. She'd respond to the department secretary's e-mail after she separated the boxes that held Richard's materials from those belonging to Professor Faber.

When she opened the attic door, Snickers dashed between her feet and into the room. Maggie had to laugh and shake her head. He couldn't resist investigating this space that was usually closed off to him. "Just don't hide in here on me. I don't want you locked in the attic when I leave."

The sun streamed in weakly through three dormer windows, not quite reaching to the far corner with its piles of stored boxes. Hitting a switch turned on the overhead lights and filled the large space with artificial illumination.

Maggie looked around. Cleaning tools leaned against a large moving box. Half a dozen heavy-duty cardboard boxes with the university's return address were carefully stacked against the wall along with a few wooden crates. The wooden crates appeared fresh and unblemished. Despite being sturdy, however, the cardboard boxes showed signs of wear and tear. She pulled them all into the middle of the room where she could more easily examine their contents. The older boxes had a mailing label with her name and address attached. *SW* was written neatly in big black letters on an adjacent side.

She studied the bold letters for a moment, then shrugged. They didn't mean anything to her. As she continued to sort the containers, she found one of the address labels was quite loose. She gently tugged at it and easily lifted away the label from an older one stuck under it on the corrugated cardboard box. *I'm lucky this box made it through the mail.* The original mailing label read *TO: Dr. Richard Watson*, with his university address, but there was no return address.

Wanting to be systematic in her hunt, she separated the wooden crates from the cardboard boxes. Since she needed a crowbar to open the crates, she started with the boxes, ripping the packing tape off of each one. Soon, she stood in a circle of open containers and tangles of sticky tape. Since it didn't matter where she began, she started with one of the newer-looking cartons.

Just as she started, however, one of the older cardboard box's flaps moved.

A mouse? She hoped not. She wasn't afraid of mice, but she didn't want to have them in the house, and she didn't want to kill them. She examined the container. It had been sealed — the mouse couldn't have gotten in through the top. She gingerly stepped around it, looking for a hole in its side. None.

The flap moved again.

Maggie grabbed a nearby duster to fend off the rodent in case it ran toward her. She backed away, eyes glues to the offending box.

The flap rose and a brown striped tail appeared. Relieved, Maggie giggled and dropped the duster.

She reached out and pushed the flap back out of the way. A pair of green eyes studied her calmly. Snickers stretched, jumped out, and rubbed against her leg.

"You silly cat. What were you doing in there?" Maggie leaned down and stroked his side. "You really are a little scamp."

Unfazed by her criticism, Snickers rubbed his face against the box he'd just popped out of.

"Well, I might as well begin with your box. It's as good as any."

A flash of white on the inside of the top flap caught her attention. What looked like a packing slip was taped in place, and it was addressed to Richard at the university. Under the address was *One (1) black-on-white Anasazi pot.*

She peered inside the container and saw a large brown envelope on top. *Confidential* was scrawled across it in what she recognized as Richard's handwriting. It lay on top of a mass of packing peanuts. She placed the envelope on the floor and brushed aside some of the protective material, exposing the rim of a large clay pot.

She shoved more of the packing material out of the way, revealing the whole rim and its design. She pulled the pot up, then tipped it on its side atop the bed of foam. She carefully turned the piece around, admiring its near perfection. No cracks, no chips. Even to her untrained eye, this extraordinarily beautiful and intact piece of pottery looked old, even ancient. She couldn't place the motif painted around the rim. However, she suspected it was from the Pueblo culture the department secretary had mentioned in her e-mail.

Was this the material the university had sent by mistake? *But then*, she wondered, furrowing her brow, *why was the original label addressed to Richard and not the professor mentioned in the e-mail?* Unless, of course, the lab assistants had merely reused old boxes when they packed things up in order to send them on to her after his death. That didn't explain the packing slip, though, which seemed to have been from when the box was originally shipped.

Maggie leaned back on her heels, contemplating the piece. What was her husband, who had focused his studies on the archaeological history of the East Coast, doing with an artifact from clear across the country?

2

Maggie moved to another old box and found it equally filled with packing peanuts. Two more ancient pieces of pottery—one vessel about nine inches in diameter and a jar just under eleven inches tall—nestled next to each other with a cardboard piece separating them from whatever lay beneath. As she reached in to remove more of the packing material, the faint ringing of her cell phone traveled up the stairs. She frowned as she remembered leaving it on the breakfast table.

Still troubled by her findings, Maggie rushed downstairs to answer the call. Reaching the kitchen, she breathlessly grabbed for the phone. The caller had disconnected. A number she didn't recognize appeared on the screen. *Oh well.* If they really wanted to talk to her, whoever it was could call back.

She stared at the device in her hand, but she wasn't really looking at her phone. Instead, her thoughts went back to the pottery she had found in the attic.

Her mind swirled with questions. Writing off the missed call as a wrong number, she grabbed the phone book and searched for the local museum curator's phone number.

She had met the friendly, outgoing Linda Martin at a conference not long ago, and they had chatted for a while about their mutual affection for the past. Linda was enthusiastic about her job as curator of the Coastal Maine Museum. The museum centered on coastal Maine's history and prehistory, but Linda was a transplant. She'd taken the curator position at the museum, met a local fellow, married, and had a son, who was currently in middle school. She now considered herself a true Mainer, but she'd been born and raised in Tucson, Arizona, where she'd developed a passion for Southwestern prehistoric art. After arriving in Somerset Harbor, she'd been delighted to find that some years ago a donor had bequeathed a small but high-quality cache of Anasazi pottery to the museum. Due to limited space, and because Southwestern traditions didn't fit into the overall theme of the museum, those pieces were usually stored away. Though Linda often put together special exhibitions at her museum, she seldom showed this collection locally. It was most often lent out to other museums doing a special show on Southwestern Pueblo art and culture.

When Maggie found the museum's phone number, she punched it into her cell phone. When a friendly voice answered, Maggie asked for Linda Martin.

"I'm Linda."

One of the advantages of a small town. You never have to go through a line of people to reach the one you want to speak with.

Maggie introduced herself by reminding Linda that they had met recently.

"Of course I remember you, Maggie. It's nice to hear from you. What can I help you with?"

"I am doing a bit of research on Southwestern pottery and remembered the conversation we had about the museum's collection. I wonder if I could come by and see it."

"Actually, we just sent several of our best pieces out on loan to a museum in California," Linda said.

Maggie's heart sank. "Oh, that's too bad."

"Are you interested in a particular group or potter family? We have some wonderful books in our shop."

"That could help," Maggie said. *Anything might be useful at this point.* "I have a few pots that I was hoping to identify by comparing them with what you have. Anything you have along with the books will help, I'm sure."

"Ah, yes. Well, if you're doing research, I can open up the museum's storage area and let you see what we have left."

"That would be wonderful." Maggie's spirits perked up again. "Is it possible for me to come over tonight? What time would be convenient for you?"

"We're not a big museum, so we all wear a lot of different hats. I will be at the main desk until closing at eight o'clock. How about then? I will have uninterrupted time to show you the pieces in the back room."

Delighted with her luck, Maggie thanked Linda and disconnected the call. She immediately grabbed a ruler and ran back up to the attic. Making sure Snickers hadn't followed, she slipped inside and shut the door behind her. She removed the pots she'd already looked at from their boxes and placed them gently on the floor. She snapped a few pictures of each one with the ruler nearby for size.

There were a handful of other similar boxes, but Maggie had too many tasks to do this morning to look through them all. Getting more information on these few pieces would do for the moment.

Back in her office, she checked the landline phone for recent calls. A number with a Vermont area code appeared on her screen, but there was no message. Assuming the call came from the departmental secretary or Professor Faber, she hit the return button.

"This is Professor Faber," a thin voice said.

Maggie introduced herself, saying that she had received the secretary's e-mail that morning. "I'm sorry, I haven't gone through all of my husband's boxes yet."

"Not to worry, Mrs. Watson."

"I am working on it," Maggie continued. She thought for a moment, then added, "My shop is participating in our town's History by Candlelight Tour this week, and I have a lot of preparations to do. Once that is over, though, I will be able to check all of the boxes the university sent. That should be next week at the latest."

"Really, Mrs. Watson, I don't want you to have to go through extra work. I am sending over my assistant, Conrad Boynton, and he will pull out my field materials. He knows what to look for. He can be there tomorrow."

Maggie drew in a sharp breath. "Is there a rush for you on getting these boxes back?" she asked. *After all, they've been sitting in my attic for a couple of years now. Why would a few extra days be a problem?* The idea of a stranger going through Richard's things bothered her.

The professor's voice broke into her thoughts. "Your husband and I were working together on a professional publication. At Richard's death, I put the project aside, but now I've been asked to participate in a special conference on the topic we were writing about. I need the pottery as soon as possible to complete my analysis. As the wife of an archaeologist, I'm sure you understand." His tone was smooth and respectful but uncompromising at the same time.

Snickers pawed Maggie's knee as if aware of her stress. She scratched his ear. "I'm afraid that isn't a good idea. I really have too many things on my plate this week. Even if your assistant came—"

"I completely understand how difficult it must be for you," the professor interrupted. "As a new senior professor at the university, I had only started working collaboratively with Richard when he passed away. His loss was a blow to us all."

Maggie's temple began to throb. She pressed her cool fingers against her head.

Professor Faber continued. "You have a lot to do, and you probably don't know the details of your husband's research. Going through all that dusty old material from the lab would create even more anxiety and stress for you. And that's what I want to avoid. My assistant is quite knowledgeable and will relieve you of all that."

Maggie bristled as he kept talking. How dare he suppose he knew about her relationship with her husband—that they wouldn't share the details of his interests? She had to restrain herself from commenting. She wasn't about to discuss her personal life with a stranger, but she became increasingly uneasy with Professor Faber's presumptions.

Finally, she ended the phone call, making no commitment and saying she would have to get back to him. Professor Faber expressed displeasure at the delay but said he'd keep in touch.

After her conversation with the professor, Maggie prepared to go out and do a few errands. Before leaving, however, she again looked out the window, checking the skies for possible rain. She spotted a silver car not far from where one had been parked earlier. She studied it. Was that car the same one she'd seen earlier that morning? She couldn't be sure. Silver cars were a dime a dozen.

By the time she slipped on a light coat to keep out the spring cold and stepped out the door, the car was gone. Maggie headed toward The Busy Bean for a coffee, checking her watch as she walked. She hoped that her good friend James Bennett would be there on his morning break. He usually stopped into the café about this time.

Entering The Busy Bean, a gust of warm air and the scent of fried eggs, bacon, sausage, biscuits, and coffee greeted her. Daisy Carter, the café's owner and friend to all, sashayed past in a striking blouse with a large pattern of brightly colored hibiscus flowers strewn over it. She held a tray of breakfast foods high on her fingertips.

Calling a welcome to Maggie, Daisy nodded toward the row of tables along the café's windows, where James was sitting at Maggie's favorite place. Maggie waved at Daisy, walked over to James, and slid into a seat across from him.

"Morning," she said, trying for a note of cheerfulness.

He started to smile at her, but then his brow creased into a look of concern. "Is something the matter, Maggie?"

She grimaced. "Is it that obvious?"

"What happened? Are you having trouble getting ready for the History by Candlelight Tour?"

Maggie wasn't surprised that his first thought was of the tour. James himself had come up with the idea to hold the event, which would open up historic buildings around town to the public. The goal was to draw more visitors to Somerset Harbor before tourist season began in earnest, boosting the local economy and giving everyone something to look forward to as they shook off winter and welcomed spring.

With the tour coming up in a few days, many of the historic home and building owners, including Maggie, were working like mad to prepare for a deluge of visitors. As a town alderman, James had made himself available to help in whatever way needed, from arranging temporary parking signs for the streets to orchestrating the flow of foot and vehicle traffic.

Maggie had thrown herself into the project, preparing both Sedgwick Manor and Carriage House Antiques—but that wasn't what troubled her this morning.

She shook her head in response to James's question. "It's something quite different entirely." She proceeded to tell him about the e-mail and the professor's offer to help go through Richard's boxes.

James let her talk, asking a few questions about why she felt uneasy with the professor's offer. She repeated that having a stranger go through her husband's personal things bothered her. Besides, Professor Faber was wrong about her not knowing about Richard's work. He had loved talking about it, and they had spent many hours discussing it.

Maggie sighed, eyes lost in the middle distance as she remembered the past and those long evenings together. One of the things she'd always treasured about Richard was his enthusiasm for his work and his willingness to share everything with her.

"But it's more than the professor not understanding your relationship, isn't it?" James asked. "Something else is troubling you."

She looked at him, nodding, appreciating his insight. "It seems odd that I can't remember Richard ever mentioning his collaborating on a professional paper with this fellow. I am positive Richard could not have been close to him because I don't know Professor Faber. I've never met him. Not even at a faculty party."

"Is it possible Professor Faber hadn't been there long enough for you to have met him?" James asked.

"Now that you mention it, he did tell me that he'd only been with the department for a short time before Richard's death." She hesitated for a moment, then continued. "Richard had also been unusually reserved and talked less about his work in the weeks before his passing." Her eyes stung. "That was a difficult time for me. I thought he was unhappy, that our relationship was—" She stopped and shook her head. "I was reluctant to approach him about his being so distant. And then he—well, now I can never ask him what was troubling him."

James reached across the table and rested a hand on her wrist. "Maggie, from all you've told me about Richard, I'm sure he was concerned about something at work, not your marriage. He probably didn't want to burden you with it. You undoubtedly wouldn't even remember feeling that way if he hadn't passed on so suddenly, leaving what was probably a small question unanswered."

Maggie stared out the window, then nodded and looked back at him. "Maybe you're right."

He smiled, squeezed her wrist, and withdrew his hand. "Now, what are you ordering this morning?"

After sharing her breakfast break at The Busy Bean, Maggie left the café feeling better. It was good to talk with someone she trusted. As she walked down the sidewalk, she continued to mull over Professor Faber's offer to go through the boxes for her. Would it spare her from rehashing the past? Should she just ignore the nagging feeling inside her about Richard's behavior in the weeks before his death?

In the end, she decided to decline the professor's proffered assistance with the missing materials. She'd go through the boxes as soon as the tour was over. She owed her best hosting job to the shop, and to James.

And going through Richard's boxes of professional papers and artifacts would give her one last opportunity to share his passions.

. . . .

After joining June in the store late that morning, Maggie consciously turned her attention to preparing for the History by Candlelight Tour. The two set up a couple of new vignettes for the occasion, including a pirate-themed child's bedroom and a stately master bedroom. They pushed and pulled furniture to the assigned areas, arranging the beds, dressers, and nightstands just so.

June filled in details in the child's room, including a set of alphabet blocks spelling out *ahoy matey* and a teddy bear sporting a patch on one eye and a red bandanna on its head. Maggie set about artfully grouping items in the master bedroom. For sparkle on a walnut dressing table, she arranged a matching set of silver candlesticks and a silver toiletry set, complete with a mirrored tray and three small jars with filigree lids.

As the two women worked, Maggie noticed a middle-aged man with thinning hair enter the shop. He stopped at the counter, where a Chinese Qing Dynasty bowl filled with individually wrapped mints sat next to a coffeepot. Taking a handful of mints, he dropped all but one into the pocket of his tan trench coat. He unwrapped the one and popped it into his mouth. Then, he proceeded to move through the shop, examining this and that, picking up and returning small objects from displays.

Watching him out of the corner of her eye, Maggie thought how easy it could be to slip small pieces into a pocket. Most antiques shops put jewelry and other high-ticket items in glass cabinets, and Carriage House Antiques was no exception. However, like Aunt Evelyn before her, Maggie preferred to have as much of her merchandise as possible presented in still-life vignettes such as the one she was currently working on.

She stepped back and gazed at the master bedroom display. It looked like someone's actual bedroom, not just a set of impersonal furniture.

Satisfied, she smiled. She preferred Aunt Evelyn's approach— placing each antique in an evocative setting to remind the customer of its original function in daily life and showing them how those pieces could still work in modern times.

Maggie made a conscious effort to stifle any concerns about shoplifters and continued trying to bring a sense of the past into the present for her customers.

All the same, the hairs on the back of her neck prickled.

3

Later that day, Maggie and June were working side by side again on another display when the Graham twins, Francine and Lydia, entered the shop. June raised a hand in greeting. Maggie smiled and came to the front.

The twins were providing Maggie with appetizers and bite-size desserts to serve at her house and shop for the History by Candlelight Tour. Maggie's first choice for catering would have been The Busy Bean, but, long before the town had decided to have this event, Daisy had committed to hosting a rehearsal dinner for a young couple. Daisy had told Maggie she couldn't refuse the bride and groom when they told her they considered her café their "special place."

As a result, Daisy recommended the twins as an alternative. The girls, as Maggie thought of the twenty-four-year-olds, were starting a new catering venture, The Maine Occasion, which specialized in traditional Maine fare, especially desserts. Serving at Maggie's home and business for the tour would be their first big opportunity.

June had been especially pleased to hear about the twins catering the event. They were about the same age as her own twins, and they had played together as children. When Maggie mentioned her decision, June's eyes sparkled. "I remember when they were all in elementary school. Their mom was always baking, and she taught them a lot. They loved being in the kitchen and creating Maine specialties even then. And now here they are, grown up and starting this catering company."

Maggie met the girls at the shop's counter. Fraternal twins, Francine and Lydia had their own distinctive personalities and appearances. Francine—petite with a head of curly, coffee-colored hair—exuded energy, talked constantly, and laughed easily. Lydia—tall with an athletic build and her auburn hair pulled back into a ponytail—offered little to the conversation while observing everything with a quiet intensity. Maggie thought they were a good balance to each other: one a people person who connected with the customer, the other a task-oriented person who made sure the business details were taken care of. She felt confident in their combined ability to handle her refreshments with flair and authenticity in the upcoming event.

Francine laid a list on the counter. "After talking with you earlier about what you would like for Friday evening, we created a custom lineup of desserts and hors d'oeuvres. We hope you like it."

Maggie read down the page: whoopie pies, Needhams, cream puffs, custard tartlets, assorted cookies, and miniature wild blueberry pies. She looked up in surprise. "Where did you get the wild blueberries?" Blueberries were harvested in the late summer. Even the local restaurants used cultivated blueberries, not wild ones, this time of the year.

Francine laughed. "We planned ahead and froze bunches of fresh and cooked blueberries for just this sort of occasion."

"That's brilliant. Cultivated blueberries are fine, but the wild are so much better," Maggie said. "And are whoopie pies those chocolate cake things with a marshmallow crème filling? I've had one before. So tasty, although somewhat sticky."

"They are a nostalgic treat for many Mainers," Lydia said. With a small grin, she added, "We will have plenty of napkins for people."

"Sounds good." Maggie looked back at the list. "What are Needhams?"

Francine smiled. "That's the second thing—or third, if you count blueberry anything—that we Mainers consider our 'down-home' dessert. It's a chocolate-dipped bar with the most surprising ingredient."

"And what is that?" Maggie asked gamely.

"It's mostly sugar, coconut, and—you'd never guess—mashed potatoes!"

Maggie stared at the dessert list. "Mashed potatoes? Do people really like it?"

"Oh yes," Francine said. "Since both whoopie pies and Needhams are considered more trouble than baking a batch of cookies, though, not many people actually make them anymore. That's why having these particular desserts on Friday will make your refreshments the talk of the town. Everyone will love it."

"Wonderful," Maggie said. "But with all these sweet things, maybe we should have some savory items as well."

"We will." Francine tapped the list below the desserts. "Biscuits and crackers with fish and crab fillings. Plus, a couple of platters of cheese, fruits, and vegetables."

"And I'll have the drinks ready to set up near the food table. Otherwise, I think everything is covered." Maggie was relieved to know she didn't have to be concerned anymore about the food for the tour. There was enough to do just with cleaning, organizing, and decorating.

The twins gathered up their papers.

"Before we go, we'd like to look around," Lydia said. "We haven't been in the shop since we were kids, and we won't have time on Friday."

Delighted at their interest, Maggie pointed them toward a few particular displays. The twins set off, Francine excitedly pointing out pieces here and there.

Maggie returned to the child's bedroom and put a few final

touches on the vignette. In keeping with a pirate theme, she included an old treasure chest that could serve as a storage area for extra blankets. June stayed at the main counter to wrap-up a sale of a French Provincial coffee table for a middle-aged couple.

Eric Clark, a college student recently hired as seasonal help, appeared from the work area to begin his shift. "Hi, boss," he said. "Where should I start today?"

"Hi, Eric." Maggie pointed toward the front counter. "Could you please go help that couple take their table to their car?"

"Sure thing," Eric said. He headed in the couple's direction.

The soft sounds of customers' voices swirled through the shop. As she worked, Maggie casually took notice of them. There were a couple with a distinct Boston accent discussing their vacation plans as they passed, a father and child she recognized as locals, and the mint man she'd seen that morning. *Was he drawn back by the bowl of peppermints?* She'd have to keep the candies on hand. Whatever it took to make a customer feel welcome.

For a short break, she joined June for coffee and invited Eric to share a cup as well. Sitting on stools behind the empty counter, she told June about the secretary's e-mail and about the call from Professor Faber offering to help Maggie go through Richard's boxes.

Eric perched on a nearby stool and listened attentively to Maggie's story. When she had finished, he enthusiastically joined the conversation.

"Native American arrowheads and stuff are really amazing," he said. "I have a small collection. Well, it's mostly my dad's. When he was young, he'd go out into the fields to find stuff, mostly broken bits of stone, but sometimes really nice arrowheads. He traded with other collectors and even bought a few. He saved his collection for me. Now I'm building on it. It's a lot of fun and could even be worth some money someday."

"That's nice," June said. "I love it when a parent can share a hobby with their child."

Eric turned to Maggie. "What kinds of things did your husband have? Do you know anything about them? How old they are? Where they came from?" His questions poured out almost faster than he could form the words.

Maggie had to disappoint him. She doubted that artifacts from Richard's own fieldwork in historical Northeastern archaeology would be in the crates. She was sure those materials would have to be kept at the lab, stored for future study, or perhaps placed in the university's small museum. Though he had raised the money to carry out the archaeological work, the materials weren't his property. As a part of the nation's history, they were to be kept in trust by the university. She had no idea what was in the wood crates—perhaps just his working tools. She would find out after Friday as she continued her search for Professor Faber's Southwestern pottery.

"I did find some lovely pots that I think are Southwestern, but I don't know enough about all of the things stored yet," Maggie said. "I'll know more after I visit Linda Martin at the Coastal Maine Museum this evening."

"Did you see that news article on a Native American artifact auction where a First American bannerstone called Sunset Glory sold for $245,000?" Eric asked. "That price broke all records. It was a gorgeous piece."

"Wow, they'd better know its provenance," June said. "What is a bannerstone, anyway?"

"Bannerstones are atlatl weights. Hunters put them on a throwing stick used to propel a spear. The atlatl gave the spear a lot of thrust, more power." Eric's voice had a note of pride at his expertise in the matter.

"Still, it's a stone. How can it be dated? And how can they

be sure it's old and not just a reproduction?" June asked.

Eric brushed his hair back off his forehead. "There are experts. I wouldn't be able to tell the difference, but I guess they can."

As Maggie listened, she noticed the mint man standing within earshot of their conversation and appearing to eavesdrop. At Eric's revelation of the value of the prehistoric artifact, he sharply stepped away and walked toward the back of the shop.

"It's my dream to find a piece as perfect as that bannerstone," Eric said, his eyes unfocused as if seeing beyond his surroundings.

"What would you do with it?" June asked.

"Oh, I'd sell it. With that much money, my father and I could have a comfortable life. No problems." He laughed at the improbability of it all. "But the likelihood of finding such a valuable stone is like being struck by lightning while standing in my living room."

. . . .

Finding a parking space on the street across from the museum proved easy at this time of night. The streetlights cast a soft glow over the sidewalk. Smaller old-fashioned post lights surrounding the museum illuminated the walkway. Maggie savored the cool air as she hurried down the path. The front doors were closed and locked for the night, so Linda had instructed her to go to the service door and ring the bell.

Maggie didn't have to wait long before the heavy oak door opened. She was greeted by a comfortably round woman with her hair indifferently tucked behind her ears and a rectangular shawl with an intricate, wandering pattern hanging loosely over her shoulders.

"How do you like living in Sedgwick Manor?" Linda asked as she led Maggie inside. "Your aunt Evelyn had a way of keeping the past while living in the present."

Surprised at Linda's use of that particular phrase, Maggie shot her a quick glance.

The woman smiled. "I knew your aunt well. We shared an interest in history and in preserving the past. She was remarkable. Always curious."

Maggie brightened. "That's something I always remember about her too."

The amiable curator led the way along a dim hallway and down a broad set of stairs to an enormous room on the lower level. Metal shelving filled its center space, and bookshelves covered its four walls. A scarred oak worktable and chairs that had seen better days sat near the stairs. The room was lit by fluorescent overhead lighting.

"You said you were interested in our Native American collection," Linda said, talking over her shoulder as she guided Maggie down an aisle defined by six-foot-high metal shelves.

"I'm interested in identifying some pottery. I believe it's Southwestern. I do have pictures of a few of the pieces." Maggie reached into her purse.

Linda stopped. "Wonderful. It'll help narrow the search. Some of those archive containers are quite heavy."

Maggie handed her the pictures she had printed out before leaving the house. Linda studied each one. "Anasazi. And these appear to be in remarkable condition." She looked up at Maggie. "Without actually seeing them, I'd say they are museum quality."

"Wow," Maggie whispered.

"Wait here. I'll get a dolly for us and then we can bring the materials I think you might benefit from seeing."

Linda returned shortly, dolly in tow. She approached the shelving and squinted at the identifying numbers on the front of each archival box. After examining a handful of boxes, she nodded and tapped one. "These are the ones you'll want."

The women lowered the containers onto the dolly and rolled them to the table. Linda handed Maggie a pair of white disposable gloves and slipped another pair on her own hands. Then she opened the boxes and carefully placed their contents on the table. Most of the bowls and pots had black geometric designs over a cream-colored base. A few pieces had an orangish-buff background instead, and even fewer bore animal figures.

Maggie ran her gaze over the surface of a large rounded pot with a narrow neck. "These are so beautiful. And look at their perfect condition after so many years."

"The Pueblo culture covers part of what is now Arizona, New Mexico, Utah, and Colorado. Most of the museum pieces are from AD 825 to as late as 1300. From the pictures you showed me, I'd say yours may date from around AD 1000 to 1200."

Maggie placed her photos on the table next to a pot Linda had unpacked and noted that they certainly resembled each other. "Maybe they're replicas?"

Linda shook her head. "These are only photographs, and I'd have to see the pieces themselves to be sure, but they seem to have signs of aging. Well-made replicas have a brighter tone to them. It's not too difficult to tell an original from a copy."

"If they're genuine, how valuable are they?"

Linda pursed her lips, thinking. "Thousands of dollars. It depends on the buyer. Even broken pieces of Anasazi pottery can sell for a few hundred dollars. Are you thinking for insurance purposes?"

"I hadn't thought that far ahead."

Linda glanced back at the photographs. "Where did you get these? How many more do you have?"

Maggie didn't want to say too much, particularly because she really didn't know a lot. The items in her attic may be what the university and Professor Faber said had been sent to her by mistake, the artifacts that belonged to Faber. But if they were the professor's, what explained the original mailing labels she found under the university's recent labels when they sent the boxes to her? The older labels and the packing slip inside were addressed to Richard at the university, not to Professor Faber. The whole situation was rather confusing.

Breathing deeply, Maggie picked up the printouts of the black-on-white pottery and slipped them into her purse.

"These belong to a friend. I told him I'd be willing to do some research on them for him," Maggie said. She liked Linda and she hated lying, but until Maggie knew more, she was hesitant about telling many people what Richard's boxes contained.

Using her phone's camera, she snapped several pictures of the pots spread out across the table, again using a ruler to indicate size. Linda packed them carefully back into their boxes as Maggie completed each shot. Finally, after thanking Linda for all her help, Maggie left the museum mulling over what she'd learned.

As she walked out into the biting night air, the nagging question of what Richard had been doing with such materials enveloped her. And who was the true owner of these precious antiquities? Richard? The professor? The university?

After meeting with Linda, Maggie had even more questions than answers. Distracted by a swirl of potential scenarios, she stepped out onto the road.

"Watch out! Car!"

A woman's voice jolted Maggie out of her reverie. Instinctively glancing up the dark street, she saw a car without headlights barreling toward her. Her heart raced as she threw herself toward the sidewalk. Her foot caught on the curb. As she stumbled forward, a pair of arms caught her and kept her from falling onto the concrete.

A *whoosh* of wind engulfed them as the car sped past.

"Are you all right?" the voice asked.

Gulping air, Maggie nodded. She couldn't speak. Her eyes remained on the pavement. One thought filled her: She could have been killed. An image of her daughter, desolate and alone, flashed into her consciousness and then was gone.

She began to shake and covered her eyes. She felt a cloth being draped over her shoulders.

"It's okay. You're okay."

Maggie reflexively moved her hand to hold the cloth and opened her eyes. Linda stood next to her.

"Thank you. If you hadn't . . ." Maggie shuddered.

"It's a good thing I left just behind you," Linda said, her forehead creased. "That guy could have hit you. And he never slowed down or stopped. It's as if he didn't even see you." She shook her head and drew up one end of the shawl so that it doubled over Maggie's shoulder. "Did you get a good look at the car? Could you identify it or see its license plate?"

Maggie shook her head. "It all happened too fast."

"I couldn't get a good look either. I was in a panic about you and wasn't quick enough to be able to identify it. Do you want me to drive you home?"

"No. It's not far and my car is right here. I'm fine."

But Maggie didn't feel fine. Troubling questions popped up and she couldn't push them aside. Why was that car coming so fast down this side road at night and with no lights on? How could the driver not see her and almost run her over? Her hands trembled from nervous energy. Breathing deeply, she forced herself to keep calm.

Finally rallying, she reasoned with herself. *Surely it was simply an accident.*

Removing Linda's wrap, she handed it to the curator with more thanks. Trying to ignore the icy feeling in her veins, she crossed the road to her waiting car, repeatedly looking both ways as she did. She couldn't be too careful.

4

Maggie woke up unsettled. As she prepared for work and walked the short distance to the shop, she thought about the previous night's close call. Since neither she nor Linda had been able to identify the car or read its license plate, she had decided not to report the incident. Besides, she had a seemingly endless to-do list to finish before Friday's tour. There was no time to speculate whether the near collision was indeed an accident— or not.

While June ran the cash register, Maggie made the rounds through the store. She wanted everything to be as engaging as possible. Reaching the pirate-themed child's room, she stood in the aisle and gazed at the display. Each antique was neatly placed in its intended spot so that the completed tableau truly resembled a kid's bedroom, albeit an unusually tidy and well-decorated one. Nevertheless, looking around, she couldn't help but feel something was missing. Chewing her lower lip in concentration, she again surveyed the scene. She stopped at the treasure chest and nodded. It needed sparkling bounty spilling out to give the scene a sense of fun.

With the tour only a couple of days away, Maggie wondered where she could get enough jewelry to make an impact without spending much. She turned toward the glass cabinet that held the shop's necklaces, rings, and earrings. *Well, I can't just drape those haphazardly about.* She walked up to the front to see if June had any ideas.

Not surprisingly, June had the perfect solution.

"Garage sale season is here, Maggie," June said with a smile. "I saw signs just this morning on my way here. Maybe you could find someone selling costume jewelry to use as props." She looked at the clock. "You might want to leave now for a good selection."

"June, you're a genius," Maggie said. "I'll go right away and be back to set things up this afternoon."

Leaving June to manage the shop and Eric to help, Maggie headed out, a woman on a mission. As she drove around Somerset Harbor looking for garage sale signs, she fondly thought back on the times she and her daughter had done the same on weekends in Bennington, Vermont. Their friendly competitions over who could find the better deal or the more ridiculous item were a highlight of Emily's school years, and their outings had often been a morale booster after Richard's death.

It wasn't long before Maggie hit pay dirt. On the second stop, she came across a shoe box full of ostentatious costume pieces: a necklace of pearls with a gem-encrusted pendant, a faux diamond tiara, fake sapphire brooches, and massive imitation gold chains and strands of pearls. After some judicious bargaining, she bought the whole box for five dollars.

Pleased with her find, Maggie started for her car. As she passed another set of tables piled high with old tools, Maggie noticed a fellow who looked familiar. Wearing a khaki trench coat and a brimmed hat, he resembled the mint-hoarding man in her shop yesterday. She wasn't sure if he was the same person, though. The khaki coat looked familiar, but it was a fairly generic style, and the hat hid part of his face.

Gripping her package, Maggie glanced at the man one more time. He had picked up a rusty monkey wrench and appeared to be closely examining it. She smiled to herself. *A fellow lover of old things.* She turned away, shoe box in hand.

Maggie returned triumphantly to Carriage House Antiques

with her glittering jewels. She'd been gone less than two hours, leaving her plenty of time to work on the display. She immediately went to the child's bedroom and cracked open the pirate chest. First, she arranged the jeweled necklaces to spill onto the floor. Then, she placed brooches and a tiara over them, as if they had fallen out of the chest. The overhead lighting caused the pendants, pins, and crown to sparkle, drawing attention as they lay among the ropes of gold and pearls. Maggie grinned. It was the final touch she needed to evoke pirates and their treasures, to set young imaginations aglow.

She crossed the child's bedroom vignette off her to-do list. She set about her other tasks, and the afternoon passed quickly.

After she and June closed the shop, Maggie rushed home to prepare for an early supper with James and his mother, Deborah. When James's mother had called earlier to invite Maggie for dinner, she said she'd been to the store and had bought a whole chicken because they were on sale, but then realized it was too much for just her and James. Would Maggie like to join them?

Deborah's invitation reminded Maggie of how her own grandmother used to ask the family over for a casual dinner. When they arrived, the dinner table would fairly groan with the weight of plates and bowls overflowing with delicious food. *Casual indeed.*

Snickers greeted Maggie when she stepped into the manor. She hung up her coat, then picked him up. "How have you been today, big guy?" she asked, scratching his neck.

He leaned into her and purred. She laughed, gave him a hug, and put him down. Within a short time, she had changed clothes, freshened up, and was on her way out. Snickers sat in the kitchen, watching her leave again with disapproval.

"Be good and guard the house," she said, and she closed the door behind her.

Maggie made a quick stop at The Singing Mermaid Floral Shoppe to pick up a bouquet of flowers. She chose a bunch of cheery yellow daffodils that heralded spring's imminent arrival, then headed to Deborah's house.

James answered the front door of his childhood home, a smile lighting up his face. "Mother's in the kitchen," he said.

She stepped into the warm foyer and offered him the bouquet. "These are for your mother."

"Beautiful," he said. "But you can give them to her yourself. Come this way."

He led her through the dining room — where a white embroidered tablecloth covered a large oval table set with gleaming china and crystal — and into the kitchen. If Maggie hadn't been hungry when she arrived, the aromas filling the kitchen certainly would have stirred her appetite.

Deborah looked up from the stove, wooden spoon in hand. The stove's heat added color to her cheeks, giving her a healthy glow.

"Maggie, how good to see you," Deborah said. "We're almost ready. James, get her something to drink, please."

"Sure. I'll get a vase for the flowers too," he said.

Deborah peered over at the bouquet in Maggie's hands. "You didn't have to bring anything, dear."

"It's the least I could do to thank you for having me." Maggie handed James the flowers. "I hope you love daffodils as much as I do."

Deborah nodded enthusiastically. "The weather has been so dreary this past week. These are just what the doctor ordered."

Maggie grinned. "I think we're all tired of winter and ready for spring."

As they settled down for dinner, they discussed Maggie's finds for the antiques shop vignettes, James's activities for the history tour, and Deborah's newest quilt design. As they finished their dessert of chocolate mousse, the dining room's Seth Thomas gingerbread clock chimed the half hour.

"It's six thirty," James said. "I'm afraid Maggie and I have to leave for our meeting at the historical society."

Deborah chuckled. "You're at so many meetings, you're almost a regular."

"I come when called," James said with a smile. An expert in restoration, he often proved invaluable when someone donated a special but damaged antique to the society's small collection. "Tonight's meeting is about the tour, so it's business and pleasure."

"I wish I could be there, but I promised Fran this quilt design would be done in the next few days, so I need to focus on it. I want it to be just perfect."

"Your designs always are, Mother," James said with pride.

Maggie glanced up at the lustrous walnut clock and sighed. It was so pleasant being here with Deborah and James. Much as she enjoyed her new life and friends, she missed the family dinners she used to share with her husband and daughter, when everyone talked about their day and what they were doing. This evening had reminded her of those simple joys.

. . . .

When Maggie and James arrived at the teal-and-rose Queen Anne that housed the Somerset Harbor Historical Society, the first floor was fully lit. Entering the building, they could hear lively chatter coming from the library.

The room's rich woodwork fairly glowed under the crystal chandelier hanging over a massive mahogany table. Ruth Harper, the society's president, presided at one end with Daisy and June on either side of her. Gathered around the ample table were other members. Fran Vosburg, the youngest member of the historical society, sat erect, her hands gently moving over a folded silk-and-wool neck scarf laid out on the table. Fran was the owner of The Quilt Cupboard, where Deborah sold her one-of-a-kind quilts. Next to Fran sat Liz Young, a counselor whose husband, David, was the pastor at Old Faith Chapel. And in the last chair perched septuagenarian Ina Linton, a petite and energetic fixture of Somerset Harbor who always knew the latest about town—thanks especially to her police scanner.

Along with the usual members, Maggie noticed a young woman she didn't recognize sitting near the two empty chairs saved for her and James. As they took their seats, James introduced them.

"Maggie, this is Connie Allen, a freelance reporter for the *Southern Maine Rural Electric Newspaper.* She'll be doing an article on our History by Candlelight Tour." He turned to Connie and said, "This is Maggie Watson. She owns Carriage House Antiques and Sedgwick Manor."

"Oh, I am delighted to meet you," Connie said, shaking Maggie's hand. "I drove past your house and shop on my way into town today. If the outside is any indication of what's inside, I can't wait to see the interiors, especially at the shop."

Maggie read the *Rural Electric Newspaper* and enjoyed their well-written articles highlighting the towns, businesses, and craftspeople in its service district. The consistently positive articles often stressed the human element in their stories. "I'd be happy to show you around," Maggie said. "You're welcome anytime. We have themed room settings to show off our merchandise. It's like taking a step back in time."

"What a fabulous idea," Connie said.

"Creating the vignettes was something my aunt, who originally owned the shop, came up with. If you come before Friday evening, you can get some good pictures of the settings, then on

Friday you could photograph the guests and later decide which works better for your article." Realizing she was telling Connie her business, Maggie added, "Or however you'd like to do it."

Connie chuckled. "I am pretty new at reporting for the newspaper. I recently graduated with a degree in journalism."

"Ah, that's a challenging field today, especially with the Internet," Maggie said.

"Yes, but I'm drawn to it just the same: interviewing people, getting just the right photograph, and putting it all together." Connie sat a bit taller and pushed her shoulders back. "I was thrilled to get a spot as a reporter with the newspaper in my home area. This is my first job, and I really want to do the best I can. I'll take any helpful hints you can give me."

Maggie pulled out her phone. "I have a couple of pictures I took today of our most recent installations. One's of a child's bedroom, and the other's a master bedroom." She brought up a snapshot of the child's room with the porthole mirror on the wall and jewels dripping out of the pirate chest. "We think it'll be fun for adults and children alike." She handed the phone to Connie for a closer look.

Connie took the phone and enlarged the picture to see its details. As she zoomed in on the chest, a strange expression came over her face. Then she zoomed out and went on to the next snapshot of the master bedroom. Handing the phone back, she asked a few questions about the furniture's style and age. As Ruth called the meeting to order, Connie whispered that she'd love to stop by tomorrow morning to get a few pictures for her article.

Maggie tucked her phone back into her purse. A picture or two of her shop in the *Rural Electric Newspaper* would be wonderful advertisement for her business. People outside of their service area also subscribed to the newspaper because of its charming and informative articles on the businesses and craftspeople in the region. But what had caused Connie's odd reaction to the photo of the chest?

The group spent the next hour or two going over old business and new, including preparations for the History by Candlelight Tour.

After the meeting, Maggie returned home. She opened the door and flicked on the lights, looking for Snickers. He had developed the habit of greeting her on her return, but tonight no plump tabby met her at the door.

"Snickers, I'm home," she called out, hanging up her coat.

No Snickers.

"I wonder where he's gone," she muttered under her breath. She walked through the kitchen and around the first floor. Finally, she found the cat in the library, sitting on her favorite chair, green eyes watching her. As she approached, she noticed that every line of his body was taut. The fur on his tail stood on end.

"There you are," she said. "What are you doing in here? Are you hiding?" Snickers didn't relax, so Maggie continued talking to him. "You know, big guy, either you're going to have to learn English, or I'll have to learn cat. And I don't have much hope for my learning cat. What's wrong?" She stroked his back and glanced around the room. Everything seemed fine in here, and she hadn't noticed anything amiss when she'd searched for him.

Nevertheless, given Snicker's unusual behavior and her sense of unease during the week, Maggie decided to check out the rest of the house.

Cell phone in hand in case she needed to call 911, she cautiously moved up the steps to the second floor and slowly scrutinized the hallway. Each room's door rested fully open, just as she had left them. She tiptoed down the hall, feeling like a prowler herself. At each door, she cautiously peered in before stepping inside and perusing the room with care. Once assured all was normal on the second story, she climbed the narrower set of stairs to the attic.

The lights for the stairway were exceptionally dim. She looked up at the light fixture. Two bulbs were out.

"Note to self," she muttered. "Replace bulbs."

The higher she stepped up the stairs, the feebler the light. Pushing down a sense of panic, she proceeded. Light or no light, she had to know if her home was safe.

Reaching the attic landing, she stared in front of her. One large, all-encompassing room filled the entire attic, and its only door appeared to be ajar. Maggie searched through her memory of her most recent trip to the attic. Had she left it open when she was up here last? She had been in a hurry. She couldn't be sure. But unlike the second floor, she usually kept this door closed so that Snickers wouldn't get in. He could easily get lost in the jumble of everything Aunt Evelyn had stored there and all of Maggie's as-yet-unopened moving boxes, not to mention the furniture and other odds and ends.

Maggie remained momentarily on the landing. She checked her cell phone and was reassured by its face, alight with her *Favorite* phone numbers. Keeping a finger over the entry for 911, she gently pushed the attic door the rest of the way open. The hinges emitted a soft squeak. She stopped, holding her breath and listening.

Nothing.

She stepped forward. The doorframe formed a protective scaffolding around her. Slowly reaching along the wall on her right, her fingers connected with the light switch. In one swift movement, she turned on the overhead lights. A brilliant white light flooded the room, expelling the darkness.

At the same time, she heard someone running downstairs and a door slam.

She hit the 911 button.

5

Less than fifteen minutes later, Officer Samantha Clayton sat on Maggie's couch, notebook and pen in hand. She was a tall, athletic woman in her midforties. In her blue uniform, she could have been a model on a police recruitment poster. Snickers joined them, curled up nonchalantly on the Persian area rug. He alternated between bathing his paws and staring at Officer Clayton.

"So, you think the intruder hid below and ran out when you went up to the attic?" the officer asked Maggie.

"Yes, but I'm pretty sure he, or she, had been in the attic," Maggie said. She sat ramrod straight on the edge of the leather wingback chair. She was thoroughly shaken. "When I was searching the rooms on the second floor, whoever it was probably slipped into a room I'd already checked when I was checking another one."

"Was anything missing? Can you tell?"

"I didn't have time to go through the house thoroughly before now, so I can't really say."

"Then what makes you think someone was up in the attic? That is, if you don't know if anything is missing?"

"I think several of the boxes I had recently placed in the middle of the room may have been moved. It didn't look like the packing materials had been tampered with, though, so I don't think the person had enough time to go digging in them."

"Good observation," Officer Clayton said, nodding. She tapped her pen thoughtfully against her notebook. "You likely disturbed the intruder before he had a chance to steal anything."

Snickers stretched and slowly sauntered over to the visitor, rubbing against her legs. Officer Clayton grinned. "He probably smells my cats."

"Ah, you're a cat person. Snickers can usually tell."

"I have two and I foster another one." She leaned over and stroked Snickers, who obligingly wiggled back and forth under her fingertips.

Maggie watched Officer Clayton with her cat. Somehow seeing the normalcy of the policewoman petting Snickers comforted her. She relaxed against the chair.

Once Snickers had decided he'd had enough and lay back on the rug, Officer Clayton continued her questioning. "What about on the first and second floor? You're sure nothing's missing?"

Maggie appreciated the pause in questioning that Snickers had provided. It had given her time to reflect on what happened and in what order. "I'm not entirely sure. I wasn't really thinking there'd been a break-in when I looked around after I got home. I just had a feeling that something was wrong. So I wanted to check everything out."

Officer Clayton stared at her momentarily, lips tight. Maggie was certain she didn't approve of her searching without calling 911. But how could she call when she wasn't even sure if something was really amiss?

"Well, if you find something's missing, you can let us know later." Officer Clayton rose from the couch. "Right now, I'll check throughout the house to see if I can find any signs of forced entry."

While the officer examined the windows and doors, Maggie went into the kitchen and prepared coffee for the next morning. Her hands shook as she scooped the coffee grounds into the filter. She put the scoop down and leaned against the counter. What was happening? This was only the beginning of tourist season. Well, actually, the season hadn't even really begun. Businesses were just now preparing for the summer crowds. *I hope this isn't a harbinger of a rise in crime this year.* She resolved to tell James about the incident. Maybe as an alderman he could do something.

Before leaving the manor, Officer Clayton stopped in the kitchen to tell Maggie she was through.

"One of the windows on the first floor appears to have been opened. Do you normally keep your windows locked?"

Maggie bit her lip, thinking. "The air was so fresh this morning. I did open a couple of windows."

Officer Clayton nodded. "From now on, always be sure everything is locked before you leave. Your home is close to the shop, and people can come around the building and not seem out of place. It's best for you to be careful." She paused. "You don't have to be afraid, just careful."

"I understand."

At the door, Officer Clayton gave a final directive. "Let us know if you see or hear anything unusual, anything at all. Never think you're overreacting. Trust your gut. Okay?"

Maggie smile weakly. "Thank you, officer. I will."

After the policewoman left, Maggie walked around, checking each window to make sure it was closed and locked. Assured that everything was secure, she turned off the lights and went to her bedroom. Snickers ran ahead and had climbed into her bed by the time Maggie reached the room. He, apparently, had forgotten his earlier anxiety. Maggie wasn't sure how long it would be before she could say the same for herself.

. . . .

After a restless night's sleep, Maggie decided to forgo her coffee at home and headed out to The Busy Bean. She wanted company.

She had barely entered the café and seated herself when Daisy, bearing coffee, assailed her with questions. She had already heard about the burglary and wanted all of the details.

"It was more of an attempted burglary," Maggie said. "From what I can tell, nothing is missing."

A strand of brown hair fell out of Daisy's highly teased hairdo and onto her forehead. She impatiently pushed it back and patted it into place. "Do you want a dog? I bet Abe Newton would loan you his Doberman for a while," she said, her eyebrows drawn together in a worried expression.

Maggie momentarily weighed the merits of a canine guard, but she didn't want her friend to think she was living in fear. To allay Daisy's concern, she said with a broad grin, "Snickers would never stand for it. A dog in his house? Never!"

Daisy let out a loud guffaw. "You're right. Sedgwick Manor is his castle. He's master of all."

"Including me," Maggie said, joining her laughter.

Daisy slid into the seat opposite Maggie. "What happened, exactly? I know Officer Clayton came out. I want all the details." Her twinkling blue eyes radiated curiosity as she rested her chin in her hand and stared expectantly at Maggie. "Come on, spill."

"All right, but there's not much to tell, really," Maggie said and went through the details of the previous night.

When she'd finished, Daisy sat back and said, "So, nothing new to add." She sighed.

It was all Maggie could do to keep from laughing again. As she'd suspected, Daisy already knew everything that happened last night. She had one of the best intelligence networks in town.

Daisy eyed Maggie's empty cup. "Let me get you breakfast and more coffee. You need it." With that, she was up and gone.

Maggie had nearly finished her eggs when the Graham twins breezed into The Busy Bean, hands loaded down with large bags. They headed straight for the counter, where Daisy greeted them. The girls emptied their bags, pulling out different types of cookies, scones, and muffins and placing them strategically on two silver trays Daisy pulled from behind the counter. Once finished, Francine lifted the overflowing platters, balancing one on each hand. Lydia took up a stack of business cards and small flyers.

"Friends," Daisy announced loudly, "as many of you may already know, Francine and Lydia are starting a new business, The Maine Occasion. Their specialties are traditional Maine desserts, scones, and breads, and they're also happy to cater events."

"Way to bring in the competition, Daisy," a stout fellow with red cheeks called out.

"Dan, honey, we're not competing—we're complementing each other," Daisy said sweetly. "And now, I give you Francine and Lydia with samples for all." She gestured toward the twins with a sweep of her hand.

The breakfast crowd clapped and hooted. The girls smiled broadly. Lydia bowed deeply and Francine held the trays high.

"Don't be shy," Daisy said, winking at Maggie when she caught her gaze. "They already have their first big event at Carriage House Antiques for the History by Candlelight Tour, so you know they're high quality. Take a cookie or two, and be sure to tell your friends about them. And if you like what you taste, you can pick up more on the tour."

The sisters took that as their cue to start walking among the tables, Francine offering samples while Lydia handed out business cards and flyers elaborating their menu.

Maggie took a sip of her coffee as she watched the girls. She smiled when Daisy returned and slipped into the chair across from her.

Daisy nodded toward Francine and Lydia. "Their parents have been close friends of Harry's and mine ever since we got married. Harry has known them forever. Their father went to school with him, and their mother was a couple years younger."

Her eyes softened. "I can't believe the twins are grown. Their parents sure are glad the girls have decided to stay close to home."

"I'm glad too. Who else would cater the tour for me since you're so busy?" Maggie teased.

"Well, if you hadn't waited until the last minute to ask, maybe I would have." Daisy stuck out her tongue, eyes sparkling with mirth.

When the twins came by, Maggie and Daisy took a blueberry scone to share. Munching on the sweet pastry, Maggie watched the café clientele as they, too, smiled and shared the girls' samples. *This is what small-town life is meant to be.*

. . . .

Fueled by coffee, breakfast, and that tasty blueberry scone, Maggie arrived at the shop at ten sharp, just as June was unlocking the front door for the day.

Maggie was glad to see that there were no customers in the store yet. Eric hadn't come in either. She pulled up a stool behind the counter and related the previous night's incident to June, who listened without comment, only shaking her head now and again.

After Maggie finished, June said, "Do you think someone had been walking around the outside of your house and simply noticed the open window? That it was a crime of opportunity?"

"I don't know. Nothing was taken, but I'm positive someone was in the attic. Richard's boxes were definitely moved. If it was a crime of opportunity, wouldn't the intruder have simply taken something on the first floor, like the silver or my TV? It's not much, but it could still be sold in a pawnshop. Why go all the way to the attic?"

June fiddled with the cloisonné pen dangling from a cord around her neck. "It's as if he was looking for something. Is that what you think?"

Maggie stared at her and nodded grimly. "There's as much chance of that as anything."

The clanging of the bell over the door heralded the arrival of a customer. Maggie smiled a welcome to a tall young fellow with brown hair casually curling around his ears. He wore scuffed loafers, and his jeans, although clean, had definitely been hard worn. His shirtsleeves were rolled up on his forearms.

"Good morning," Maggie said. "If there's anything you need, just let us know."

"Actually, I'm looking for Mrs. Maggie Watson," he said.

"That's me. Can I help you?"

"I'm Conrad Boynton," he said, offering his hand. "Professor Faber's assistant."

Maggie was stunned. Hadn't she told Professor Faber not to send his assistant? She couldn't quite remember her exact words. She hadn't agreed to his coming at the time of their call, she knew, but Professor Faber may have taken her lack of answer as an opening to send Conrad. Obviously, Faber was in a hurry.

Maggie grasped his outstretched hand and gave it a firm shake. "The professor did say he'd be sending an assistant, but I'm afraid I wasn't really expecting you. Do you also specialize in Southwestern prehistoric cultures?"

"I've done fieldwork with historic and prehistoric sites in both the Midwest and the West," Conrad said. "Professor Faber picked me as his assistant two years ago when I started my PhD program. I'm collaborating with him on some projects, and he promised that we'd write papers together for a couple of professional meetings and for at least one publication. So it looks like I'll be specializing in the Pueblo cultures of the Southwest."

Maggie listened carefully to his explanation. She knew he was bragging by telling her Professor Faber chose him out of any number of graduate students to be his assistant, insinuating it was going to set him on the fast track to his degree as well as give him status within the archaeological community. Obviously, he considered being Professor Faber's assistant important to his career.

"Well, unfortunately, Professor Faber has sent you too early," Maggie said. "I have a major event tomorrow and will not be able to go through Richard's boxes until afterward. I don't think I'll be able to have anything for you until next week."

Conrad tilted his head to the right and, squinting slightly, rested his steel-gray eyes on her for a moment before replying. "Professor Faber told me you might be hesitant about my taking the artifacts back to the university laboratory."

His cold eyes made Maggie feel like an insect being examined under a magnifying glass. Not to be intimidated, she held his gaze. "I told him I would get to it soon. The department secretary just sent me an e-mail about this earlier this week. But I have a business to run, and going through the boxes will take more time than I have right at the moment. I'm sorry about the university's mistake, but it's been years. I'm sure the professor can wait another couple of days."

Conrad's gaze roamed around the room. "You have quite a shop here. I guess you sell all kinds of antiques, from the recent past to the prehistoric past."

She didn't know why, but somehow his comment felt more like an accusation than a simple description of what her antiques shop—or any antiques shop for that matter—might sell.

Maggie cleared her throat. "Most of what we have comes from the nineteenth and twentieth centuries. Once in a while, we have something earlier than that, but it's rare."

"Do you handle First American artifacts?"

"We do have one local fellow who has quite a collection of arrowheads—"

"Projectile points," he corrected automatically, using the standard archaeological description.

His interruption irritated Maggie. She was now in the habit of using the common terms, the terms her customers would use and understand. "—And who," she went on, ignoring him, "often brings some in to sell. They go pretty quickly."

"Yes." He studied her cash register, frowning. "It's a problem. Too many pothunters around, messing it up for legitimate archaeologists," he said, straightening his shoulders. "All they want is a projectile point, a hammerstone, a piece of pottery. They go out and destroy sites just looking for a prize. They don't care about the scientific information they ruin by randomly digging here and there. Professor Faber is always on the watch for those kinds of problems in the Southwest. Some unscrupulous collectors will even buy pots stolen from protected lands."

Maggie bristled. "The arrowheads," she said, using the term purposely, "are from this gentleman's farm. He has the right to do with them as he wishes."

Conrad sneered. "Certainly." He turned toward the rows of antiques. "Since I'm here, I guess I'll have a look around." With that, he stalked off into the shop's interior.

Without comment, June opened her eyes wide at Maggie.

Maggie grimaced. "I simply can't get to those boxes now." She thought for a moment, gazing in the direction Conrad had gone. "I think to be safe, I'm going to move all of Richard's things, every box and crate, over here to the shop's storage room today. Having all of them together will make it easier to go through . . . when I have time."

"Eric can help you bring them over." June glanced at the clock. "He's late today. That's not like him. I wonder if he's sick."

June had no sooner finished speaking when the bell chimed over the door. Eric, looking utterly disheveled, trudged into the shop. His eyes were puffy from an apparent lack of sleep.

Maggie couldn't help but wonder why he looked so tired and scruffy this morning. What was he up to last night in this town that usually turned in so early? She wanted to ask, but his hooded eyes begged her not to.

First someone breaks into Sedgwick Manor, and now my energetic assistant looks like he hasn't slept in a year. What is going on? An unpleasant idea poked the back of her mind.

Could the events be related?

6

Maggie took an old mug from a low shelf, filled it, and handed the black coffee to Eric as he reached the counter. "You look like you'll need this before you start the day," she said.

He accepted the cup and leaned heavily against the old wooden countertop. He gingerly sipped the hot liquid. "I'm so sorry I'm late, Maggie."

"Don't worry about it. Just don't make it a habit."

"I'm not used to late hours," he said. "I'm an early riser."

"What kept you up so late? Hot date?" June asked, grinning.

"No such luck." Eric smiled back wanly. "I'm taking three college classes online. The hours are flexible, but the workload is still tough."

"It's nice that you can take the classes from home, at least," June said.

"It is handy. I'm saving money by taking some community college classes before I finish up my degree at the university." Eric pushed his hair out of his eyes. "One of my classes has its first test today. I couldn't sleep and ended up studying all night."

"It must be hard to get back into the school habit," Maggie said. "How long has it been since you were in school?"

Eric sipped his coffee. "I went straight into the military as soon as I graduated from high school. That was one of the best decisions I've ever made. I learned a lot." He paused, eyes staring down at his hands. "Since coming home, though, I've found that my experience won't help me get a job in the field I want." He looked up. "No offense, of course. I really like working for you here."

"None taken," Maggie said with a smile.

"I need a college degree to move ahead, but I also need to stay here in Somerset Harbor where I can help my dad since he doesn't get around too well. Even an hour commute is too much if it's several times a week."

"Your father must really appreciate having you live at home with him," June said. "And taking the required core courses at a community college is cheaper than attending a university."

Eric's face lit up. "Not only that, but besides the two basic courses, I'm also taking a pretty amazing First American prehistory class that is only offered online. So far, we've been covering the Southwestern part of the United States. The Pueblo people were amazing." His eyes shone as he related details of what he'd been studying.

Maggie smirked inwardly at his enthusiasm for a topic that, at least for the past few days, had caused her nothing but grief.

Eric drained his coffee. "Did you say you had some Southwestern pottery here? I'd love to see the real thing, not just a picture in a book. That would be awesome."

"As a matter of fact, I need your help this afternoon moving all of Richard's boxes that are in the manor's attic over here to the shop. I want to have all of his things in one place."

Eric's eyes lit up. "Sure!"

Just then, the shop bell rang, and Connie entered with a camera bag hanging heavily over one shoulder and a notebook clutched in her hand. Following directly behind her were a couple of women who looked like a mother and her thirtysomething daughter. The three newcomers clustered together at the counter.

Maggie greeted Connie, and June spoke to the customers, who were hunting for period pieces to decorate the younger woman's new home. At the same time, the phone rang.

June took the call but soon held the phone out for Maggie.

"It's Lydia Graham. She has a question for you about food for the tour."

"Excuse me—this will only take a minute," Maggie said to Connie as she took the phone.

Connie smiled warmly. "Don't worry. I'll just wander around."

Maggie wanted the reporter to receive special treatment, so she quickly introduced her to Eric. "Eric, you know a lot about our special displays. Why don't you take Connie around?" She looked back at Connie. "He can answer any questions you might have."

Eric grinned broadly. "Follow me." The pair headed toward the bedroom displays.

Lydia, it turned out, was just calling to ask what color cocktail napkins Maggie would prefer.

"White is fine," Maggie said. "Thanks for checking. I'll see you tomorrow." As she hung up the phone, a voice came from behind her.

"Always busy, aren't you?"

Maggie swiveled around and found herself looking into the startling blue eyes of Ina Linton. Today, she wore a light russet-colored jacket over a beige turtleneck and brown tweed pants. A perky dark brown felt hat sat on her cottony white hair.

"Ina, how good to see you. What brings you in?"

Ina raised her eyebrows and cast a quick, secretive glance at the other customers, then looked back at Maggie. "I would like to ask you about a walnut table," she said rather loudly, winking conspiratorially.

Her behavior made Maggie smile. What was Ina up to?

As soon as they were out of earshot of the people gathered around the counter, and with Eric and Connie nowhere in sight, Ina took hold of Maggie's arm and stretched up to whisper into her ear. "I heard about last night's burglary. Through my police scanner."

Maggie wondered how many other people Ina might have told about the incident. Was she Daisy's information source?

Privacy was often at a premium in a small town.

"Yes," Maggie said. "It was a shock."

"You poor dear. I'm sure you told Officer Clayton everything you could, but I came by to let you know that I'm available to help in any way I can." Ina dug around in her oversize purse. "Ah, here it is." She drew out a big black flashlight and held it out to Maggie. "I want you to have this. It's a bit expensive, but I think it's worth it. I ordered one for myself and a second one just in case."

She didn't say what the "in case" was, and Maggie didn't ask.

When Maggie hesitated, Ina said, "Go ahead. Take it."

Maggie accepted the gift, which proved to be unexpectedly heavy. She already had several flashlights of varying sizes and didn't particularly want something quite this heavy when any of the others would do. However, she also didn't want to hurt Ina's feelings.

"How nice. Thank you." Ina often mystified her, but this was even stranger than usual. Maggie set the weighty flashlight on the counter.

Ina picked it up again. "It's called a tactical flashlight. It has an exceptionally strong beam and even a strobe function. See?" She turned on the light and aimed it at a dark corner. The area lit up, and the light flashed rapidly as if they were in a dance club. "This is for nighttime intruders. It throws them off-balance. If you shine it directly into their faces, they won't be able to focus on you, giving you time to run away."

"How clever," Maggie said.

Taking the light from Ina, she experimented with it, figuring out how to access the different modes. "Thank you again," she told her friend. "Nothing was taken, and it was probably just an opportunistic break-in as opposed to a premeditated one, but I feel much better with this. I'll keep it close."

Ina frowned slightly. "See that you do," she replied gruffly. "And you really should be better about keeping your windows closed and your doors locked."

"I know," Maggie said. Changing the subject, she added, "Have you seen the vignettes we've set up for the History by Candlelight Tour tomorrow?"

As Maggie guided Ina toward the child's room, she saw Eric and Connie standing with their shoulders touching, engaged in a deep conversation. At the sound of the women's approach, however, the two hastily separated.

Camera in hand, Connie beamed at Maggie. "This is quite charming. I especially like the jewels. I'm also fascinated by that display." She gestured to the nearby dining room, which was set with fine Wedgwood china and glowing silver, as if for a formal dinner party. A large bouquet of flowers in a cut crystal vase completed the scene. "Eric was about to take me over there."

"I'm glad you're enjoying the shop," Maggie said. *And our fine young employee.*

As Connie and Eric moved away, Maggie turned her attention to Ina, who was walking around the pirate-themed display. Ina ran her fingertips over the dresser's smooth, dark wood. Glancing into its mirror, she rearranged her hat. She stepped around the large chest of drawers and examined a pirate's hat hung on a hook in the wall near a ship's porthole that had been transformed into a small mirror. She peered into it and touched her hair lightly, pushing the curls up a bit.

Maggie joined her.

"Clever, very clever," Ina said, pointing to the wall. "Your pirate and nautical theme will be popular with a lot of parents and their children. Who doesn't fondly remember Robert Louis Stevenson's story of Long John Silver?" She chuckled as she walked over to the pirate's chest with its overflowing jewels.

"You even have stolen treasures. What a whimsical touch."

"Thanks," Maggie said. "We had a lot of fun putting this room together."

"Where did you get those jewels?" Ina asked. "I have some friends who make the most creative pictures out of old junk jewelry."

"I found them at a garage sale I went to yesterday, just down the road. They really are perfect. I was so lucky to find them as quickly as I did. And I only paid five dollars for everything!"

As Maggie was speaking, she heard a clank of metal on porcelain. She glanced over at the dining room setting.

Connie was blushing. "Sorry, I dropped a fork on the plate."

Maggie waved her words away. "Don't worry. It happens all the time." Then she pivoted back to Ina. "What's wrong, Ina? You look disappointed."

"I was hoping you'd found a source for the costume jewelry that might have more stock. It's getting harder and harder for my friends to find as much as they need for their work."

Maggie grinned. "They may be the reason my collection of vintage costume jewelry is so low. I'll be sure and tell you if I find any more so you can tell your friends. It's good to know what people are especially looking for."

Ina stared down at the jewels, mouth pursed.

"Are you okay?" Maggie asked.

"It's more like, are *you* okay?" Ina said. "This vignette is fun and playful, but your experience last night wasn't."

Back to this again? Maggie gave her a reassuring smile. "I promise, nothing is going to happen. Even Officer Clayton said she thought the intruder was an opportunist who happened to see my window was open." Maggie admitted to herself that she was stretching the truth a little. The officer had merely said it was one possible scenario, not the only one. "I am going to be much more careful. Don't worry."

Ina scrutinized Maggie's face. "Let me know if there is anything I can do to help. And keep that flashlight with you." She headed toward the door, saying over her shoulder, "I don't want to hear about you on the police scanner again."

Maggie couldn't help but laugh. "You and me both."

Returning to the front as Ina left, Maggie recognized a couple examining the fine silverware set out on a walnut Italian Renaissance dining table. The woman wore a short, puffy jacket, and the man, a long, tan topcoat. Raking through her memory bank, Maggie recalled that this same couple had been in the shop on Tuesday and had bought a French Provincial coffee table. They seemed to be meandering down the aisle, not really looking for anything specific.

Maggie stepped up to the couple. "May I help you?"

As if startled by her attention, the woman blurted out, "No, we're in town for a day or two and are just enjoying the shops." She nearly dropped the serving spoon from the Buccellati dinner set she'd been examining.

Probably checking to see if the set is sterling silver or not.

"Not all of the businesses seem to be open," the man smoothly interjected. "We're from South Carolina and didn't realize that so many places closed down completely for the winter. We were going to head back early, actually, but the woman who runs the B&B we're staying at told us about the History by Candlelight Tour, so we thought we'd stay long enough to check it out. We're just killing time until then." He grinned a little apologetically.

"The tour will be well worth your time," Maggie said. "How long have you been in town?"

"Oh, we drove in on Tuesday," the woman said, her tone more relaxed this time.

Her companion nodded. "That's right. We saw your shop and had to stop." He looked down at the woman. "That was

Tuesday, wasn't it, darling? Time goes so fast." He turned his grin back on Maggie. "Do you have any suggestions for places we should be sure to check out before we leave? I always trust local opinions on that."

Maggie recommended The Busy Bean as a place to eat and told them about a couple of nearby historical landmarks.

The man listened. "We've driven around to nearby towns, but we missed those sites. Thanks for letting us know about them."

Pleased that she could help orient the couple to her town's unique features, Maggie wished them well, then continued walking through the shop's aisles. She was looking for Connie and Eric. Eventually, she found them in the far back, near the workroom door.

Connie saw her first and hurried over. "Thank you for the chance to come around today when there are fewer customers than there will be during the tour."

"You're welcome," Maggie said. "I hope Eric has been able to answer your questions."

"Oh yes. He's been really helpful." Connie smiled over at him, then rested her hand lightly on her camera. "I've been able to get a lot of good shots of the displays by themselves. Tomorrow, I can concentrate on getting people browsing."

As they walked to the front of the shop, Connie continued talking about how she liked the store's distinctive approach to displaying antique pieces. When they passed a glass cabinet full of big-ticket items, Connie asked if Maggie ever sold prehistoric antiques.

Maggie found the question odd, considering they'd just been discussing the historical displays and that there weren't any prehistoric artifacts in the store. She looked back down the aisle to where Eric was working, emptying a box of candles June planned to place around the shop for the tour.

What had they been talking about so secretively before Maggie joined them?

. . . .

When customer traffic died down later in the afternoon, Maggie asked Eric to come to Sedgwick Manor and help her move Richard's boxes from the house's attic to the shop. Everything she could do ahead for the tour was done, and last-minute preparations would have to wait for tomorrow. With a little break in her busyness, she decided now was as good a time as any to bring all of her husband's boxes and crates to a single location.

As they entered the foyer, Eric's eyes went immediately to the crystal chandelier suspended above the staircase. "Whoa," he said. "That's amazing! I've never been in a mansion before." Eric followed Maggie as she climbed the steps to the second floor and then led him down the hall. "It's a far cry from the army barracks."

"I'm not sure I'd necessarily call it a mansion. But come to think of it, if I hadn't visited my aunt and uncle as a child, I probably would never have seen anywhere this lovely either."

"Takes a lot of money to make someplace look this nice. Me and Dad just share a little old place in the rough part of town." Eric's voice was innocent enough, but Maggie heard longing behind his words.

"You're a hard worker, Eric," Maggie said as they reached the attic stairs. "And you're young. If you do well in school, you'll find the right path for yourself. And who knows? Maybe it'll lead you to a home you like just as much as mine."

"I'll probably be paying my dad's medical bills until I'm fifty," he said as they reached the attic. "Parkinson's is pretty expens—hey, is that one of those pots?"

Eric pointed to a box Maggie had opened the other day, which sat in the center of the attic floor.

"Oh, yes, it is," Maggie said.

"Can I look at it?" Eric moved toward the box, craning his neck to see inside.

"Well, the curator at the local museum recommends protective gloves for handling these things, so we'd need to prepare properly."

"Oh yeah, I understand. I'll just peek in, if you don't mind."

"Sure, Eric." Maggie was charmed by his youthful enthusiasm.

"Man, how amazing is this thing?" Eric maneuvered around the box so he could see the pot from every angle. "Where did you say this came from again?"

"I don't really—I can't say. Mostly because I don't really know."

"Wicked."

Maggie sighed. "We'd better get to work so we can get done before dark. We can each move the lighter boxes and then work together on the heavier or more awkward ones. Sound like a plan?"

"Sure thing, boss."

Maggie and Eric moved the containers from the attic to the driveway, then loaded them into June's SUV, which she had happily offered for the task. It only took two trips to transport all of the containers from the manor to the shop, where they piled everything in the center of the upstairs storage area.

Once the last box was in place, Eric put his hands on his hips. "Bet it feels good to have that job done."

Maggie nodded. "I'm glad you could help. It's getting late, though. You'd better clock out and head home."

"Yeah, I've got a lot of studying to do," Eric said. "Good news is that tonight's Dad's turn to cook."

Maggie smiled at the genuine affection Eric showed for his father, and she immediately thought of her daughter. *Maybe it's time to surprise Emily with a midweek call.*

7

Maggie woke to spring mists sweeping in and out of the bay, as if playing with the sun. Soon patches of brilliant blue sky began to dominate, softened by puffy cumulus clouds.

An insistent *meow* from a certain tabby reminded her that it was time for breakfast. She hopped out of bed, dressed, and scooted down to the kitchen.

After a cup of coffee and a slice of homemade bread toasted and smothered with strawberry jam, she headed over to the carriage house. Today was the big day. The History by Candlelight Tour would begin at seven that evening, just after the sun went down.

Arriving at the shop just past eight, Maggie found the lights on. As she closed the door behind her, June stepped into view, arms full of white-on-white embroidered tablecloths with bands of lace sewn on their edges. Maggie called out a greeting.

"I think we have just enough of these for the refreshment and drink tables in both the shop and the manor," June said, plopping the pile of fabric onto the counter. "The rental company will be here around noon with the tables. The twins called and left a message saying they'd be here after closing to set up for the evening."

Maggie picked up a dusting cloth and began making the rounds, moving through their morning cleaning checklist as quickly as she could before opening time.

When Maggie went to unlock the door at ten, she found a collection of people visiting with each other outside as they waited for the shop to open. She welcomed them in along with Eric, who had arrived for his shift.

"Good morning, Maggie," he said. "I remember all my jobs for today. I'll just jump right in so we can get things ready."

"Thanks, Eric."

The patrons spread out to browse throughout the store. Maggie recognized some returning customers, including a family with young children. After getting their little ones past the candy bowl without incident, the parents made a beeline for the new pirate-themed vignette. Maggie could hear the excited voices of the children as they reached it.

Maggie also recognized a lone male figure who separated from the group after they entered the shop. It was the mint man. He wore a taupe jacket over sharply pressed blue jeans. His thinning but neatly trimmed hair was swept to the side, revealing a receding hairline. Maggie wondered if there was an expensive item he had his eye on, prompting him to return to the store again. As he passed the candy bowl, he automatically grabbed a handful, dropping the red-and-white striped discs into his pocket.

Maggie wandered around the shop, dustcloth in hand, keeping an eye out for anyone who needed assistance. At the dining room display, she recognized a familiar head of chestnut hair. Connie bent over the table setting, noting the pieces and taking close-up photographs. Maggie was about to go over to her when the reporter moved away, stopping a middle-aged couple. Within moments, the three were engrossed in a conversation.

As the morning progressed, Maggie stayed on task with Eric by her side for assistance. He told her about his First American course with enthusiasm.

"I get to go on a real archaeological dig this summer," he said. "It's an awesome opportunity."

"How wonderful. How did you find out about it?"

"It's all through the course I'm taking." He expelled a

frustrated burst of air and added, "I can go *if* I can swing the fee. It's really expensive, at least for me. But I'll manage somehow."

Maggie nodded. Even though she was distracted by preparations for tonight's event, his excitement stirred memories. It reminded her of how involved Richard's students had been when they worked on his summer digs. They remained enthused even later in the year, when they spent hours back at the university lab doing the boring but necessary job of cleaning and cataloging the artifacts—often simply broken pieces of glass, shards of pottery, and bits of metal—they'd dug up during the summer.

"I collect from around here, of course," Eric continued. "My dad and I used to go out together. Walking over a freshly plowed field is the best time to find arrowheads. We know where there are sites that no one else knows about."

"Do the landowners let you keep whatever you find?" she asked.

He bobbed his head. "Some do." He looked down.

Maggie knew that look. *Avoiding eye contact because there's something he doesn't want to say.* She thought she had an idea what that was: Other landowners probably never knew they searched for artifacts on their land. Eric and his dad probably just picked up whatever they wanted from wherever. *In the past, most people didn't value Native American artifacts, not the way they do today.* Today they were worth real money.

As Eric kept talking, Maggie began to have an uneasy feeling. *Is this healthy enthusiasm or an obsession?* A sense of doubt began to build. Should she have let him help her with Richard's boxes? It was true that some were quite heavy—paper, pottery, and stone all weighing a lot—but she could have handled it alone. At the same time, having someone else there had been a huge help.

She paused and looked around the store as more unbidden memories of Richard's past digs slipped into her mind. She found herself smiling. Those had been such good times. Sighing, she glanced at her assistant and decided not to worry about Eric just now. Besides, they had to finish getting ready for the history tour. They were almost done.

When Maggie and June had finished all their projects around the shop, they made a last-minute supply list for the evening's event.

"I'll run out and grab these things," Maggie said.

"Eric and I will hold down the fort," June said with a smile.

Maggie passed The Busy Bean as she ran her errands. Glancing in the window, she noticed that the café was unusually quiet. It was midmorning, between the rush of the breakfast and lunch crowds. Taking an impromptu break, she pushed the café's door open and entered its warm atmosphere. The only customer in the dining room was an older woman. Engrossed in an open book, she sat reading while slowly munching some toast.

Maggie looked around. Normally Daisy, with her effervescent personality, greeted customers with a hearty welcome. She bestowed her warmth on everyone, whether a well-known friend or a stranger. A former beauty queen and transplant from Georgia, she brought her larger-than-life version of Southern hospitality with her.

Today, only the smell of coffee and fried breakfast foods greeted Maggie. Jenny, Daisy's main waitress, was carrying a tray of salt, pepper, and sugar refills to each of the cheery yellow tables. She looked up and called across the room, "Hi, Maggie. Daisy's in the kitchen trying out a new dessert recipe. I'll be with you in a minute."

Maggie strolled over to the young woman. "Daisy already serves an impressive variety of pastries. What is she concocting now?"

"A bunch of customers have asked for whoopie pies and Needhams. Especially out-of-towners looking to try something 'authentically Maine.'" Jenny put air quotes around the last two words with a broad grin. "Anyway, she's thinking it might be good to add them to our menu."

"I don't believe I know of another café that carries them," Maggie said. "The Graham girls are making them to serve at my shop tonight, though."

"Famously traditional, but hard to find," Jenny said. "That's why Daisy wants to serve them here. Personally, I think Needhams are weird."

Maggie looked toward the kitchen. "I thought she had that rehearsal dinner to prepare for tonight."

"Sounded like she was all caught up on that and thought she'd work on the whoopie pies for a while."

"And how's she doing with this project?"

Jenny shrugged and smiled. "Your guess is as good as mine. Go on back. I'm sure she'd love to see you."

When Maggie entered the hot kitchen with its sparkling stainless steel stovetop, oven, and commercial refrigerator, it wasn't hard to spot the café's owner. Against this commercial perfection, Daisy provided an intense infusion of form and color. She stood over a cookie tray, scoop in hand. A mixer whirled near her. She wore black pants spotted with large splotches of flour and an oversize hot-pink blouse under a white apron. Her bouffant hairdo added inches to her height, but Maggie had seen it taller.

"Hi, Daisy," Maggie said, raising her voice over the mixer's noise.

Daisy glanced up and waved her over.

"Hi, sugar," Daisy said. "I'm whooping it up with whoopie pies!" She leaned toward Maggie, raising an ice-cream scoop high in the air. "If you're good, you can have one of The Busy Bean's first ever." With that, she dipped into a bowl of dark chocolate dough, shoveled out an even amount, and dropped it onto a cookie sheet, forming the final brown mound identical to five others already waiting. Picking up the tray, she opened the oven door directly behind her and slid it in.

"Beats me why these things aren't sold all over the place. People always ask for them. I don't see what's so difficult." She set the timer for thirteen minutes. "Last batch to bake."

Maggie squinted suspiciously at the mounds cooling on racks. "What I can't figure out is why are they called pies? They look like flattened cupcakes."

"That's one of their mysteries. Whoopies have two layers of this luscious chocolate cake and a sinfully rich marshmallow crème filling."

Daisy turned off the mixer and passed a spatula around its sides, pushing the glossy white filling into the bowl's center. She passed the spatula to Maggie. "Go ahead. Try this. You'll see why these little darlings are so popular. But be careful. That marshmallow crème is some sticky stuff."

The spatula slipped as Daisy handed it to Maggie, who missed the handle. Maggie grabbed for it and caught it in the middle of the filling. A gummy white glop covered her fingers. She laughed and licked off a taste. "That's delicious. It's very sweet, though."

Daisy grinned. "I'm glad you like it. The cakes dull that sweetness and create the perfect balance." She nodded toward the industrial sink nearby. "You can wash that off your hands over there."

Maggie cleaned her hands, then came back to watch her friend work.

Daisy flipped half of the puck-shaped cakes upside down. "Hmm, these are sticky to the touch too." She wiggled her fingers at Maggie. Brown bits of cake stuck to her fingertips. She picked up a long, narrow spatula, took a dollop of filling, and plopped it onto the overturned cake. The cake moved as she gently spread the filling over it, so she tried to hold it still. Brown crumbs dotted the sides of her pure white filling. She frowned and shook her head.

"Don't want that. Looks sloppy." Daisy did another one and got the same result. "This will never do," she mumbled. Quickly rinsing her hands, she took a plastic piping bag, fitted it with a large open tip, and filled it with the marshmallow mixture. She piped a layer of filling onto one of the overturned cakes.

Daisy stepped back and smiled. She didn't need to touch the cake and the white of the filling was pristine. "There. Can't beat a good woman," she said gleefully, then started piping the snowy mixture onto the next cake.

Maggie noticed a bit of filling leaking out above the bag's metal tip, but before she could say anything, the bag burst and marshmallow crème went all over the countertop, the nearby mixer, and a couple of the mini-cakes.

Daisy's eyes opened wide as she looked at the escaped globs of sticky filling. Then she let out a hoot. "What a mess. Now I see why people would rather buy these things than bake them."

"The twins must have some tricks up their sleeves if even you can't perfect these treats."

Daisy sighed. "I'd probably be better off contracting with those girls to make them for the café."

Maggie helped her clean up the gummy mess. As they were scrubbing, the timer went off.

"Saved by the buzz," Daisy said as she removed the mini-cakes from the oven. "Almost forgot about the tops."

Finally, everything was clean, the last of the cakes were cooling, and Daisy had successfully piped the filling onto the overturned chocolate confections.

"Last step is putting the top on," Daisy said. "Easy-peasy." But when she picked up a minicake, her fingertips left marks in its tacky surface. She let out a frustrated growl and grimaced at Maggie. "People certainly won't want fingerprints on their dessert." She took a broad spatula to pick a cake top up, but she still ended up creating fingermarks on the side as she slid the cake off the utensil.

Finished, she stepped back and looked at her whoopie pies, clearly not happy.

"What's wrong? They don't look too bad," Maggie said.

"Every recipe I've read says I should now wrap each one individually in a plastic wrap. They already have fingerprints on them. Once I cover them in plastic, the plastic will cling to the tops and bottoms of the cakes, and they'll fall apart when the customers unwrap them." She scowled. "This is not worth it. I can't serve my customers this stuff, traditional or not." She glanced over at Maggie. "And I thought these were the easier of the two classic Maine desserts. Needhams apparently need a lot of room to make correctly and much more attention than I can give, what with all the other desserts and cooking we do here. I think I'll stick with my usual stuff and leave this fancy nonsense to Francine and Lydia."

Maggie gave her friend's shoulder a quick, reassuring squeeze. Daisy wasn't used to struggling in the kitchen.

Daisy sighed and sat on a stool near the work counter. "And here I thought I could fit this project in before we prep for the rehearsal dinner tonight," she said. "I was really fooling myself. What a waste of time."

"Oh Daisy, don't fret," Maggie said. "People love your other pastries. The Busy Bean has never had these before. No one will expect or miss them."

Daisy nodded, but Maggie read unhappiness at this failure written all over her face.

. . . .

Back in the shop, Maggie found that she was restless. She knew it wasn't simply in anticipation of the History by Candlelight

Tour. After her third peek at a nearby wall clock, she finally admitted that Richard's boxes were calling to her. Telling herself she'd only check one, she slipped into the upstairs attic.

The pile of crates she and Eric had brought over yesterday rested in the middle of the space. She glanced at them, and then she set about finding the boxes of Richard's that had been in the shop attic since she'd moved in. It didn't take long to locate some of them along a side wall, though she knew there were more scattered throughout the room.

Maggie grabbed the closest box, a cardboard carton with a handwritten *SW* on its side. The tape sealing it was loose, as if it had already been removed and pressed back in place. She pushed the upper flaps open. Inside, she discovered four smaller pieces of pottery that were similar to those she'd examined in the manor house attic.

Also like the boxes she'd opened at the manor, a brown envelope had been tucked inside. Large, black letters declared the contents to be *Confidential*. She opened it and pulled out a sheet of yellow lined paper. A cryptic list of initials, dates, dollar amounts, and pottery descriptions ran across its page in neat rows and columns.

She stared at the paper. The descriptions matched the pots in the box. The handwriting was Richard's. Had he packed and cataloged the pieces? But what was he doing with them, and why were they hidden away in these boxes? His area of interest was the Eastern United States. He never mentioned working on Southwestern prehistoric materials. This must be what had been sent by mistake.

Maggie examined the original label, which was addressed to Richard at the university. The return address was a post office box in Texas, and there was no obvious clue as to the identity of the sender.

Her earlier questions reverberated through her. Why would

these materials have been sent to her husband? Even if they were working on a professional paper together, this didn't make sense. The label held only Richard's name, not Faber's. If Faber was the expert, he would have the contacts they needed, so the materials should have been sent to him, right? He would have been the one trusted with artifacts like this, not Richard, who would have been an unknown in this field.

Maggie shook her head and returned the paper to the envelope and put it in the box.

June called up the stairs that she and Eric had finished their checklist, and she wanted to know what else Maggie needed for the evening.

As she rose to return to the shop, Maggie found another question crossing her mind: Who had opened the box? Eric had access to the room, so he could have done it. But when? She thought back to his comments about needing money and his strong interest in the monetary value of Native American artifacts.

Maggie closed the box's flaps and carefully placed the container under other cardboard cartons, turning the initials toward the wall.

She rushed downstairs and told Eric she'd need him to help her in Sedgwick Manor tonight, assuring him that June could handle the tour of the shop. She wanted him close so she could keep an eye on him.

Back on the sales floor, immediate tasks inundated her, and she spent a lot of time putting out small fires. Maggie was focused on the computer screen at the counter, trying to track down a lost package for an out-of-state customer, when she heard a familiar voice. "So tonight is your big affair."

She looked up into hard eyes the color of stone. Conrad Boynton. If someone else had said this, it would have sounded friendly. His words, however, contained a note of condemnation—or suspicion.

"Hello, Conrad."

"I understand both of your buildings will be in the tour," he said, leaning against the counter.

"Yes, Sedgwick Manor and its carriage house are both historic structures." She looked closely at him. He was wearing the same jeans with a different shirt from the other day. "You decided to stay in town?"

"You said you'd be ready in a few days, after your big event."

Maggie didn't understand why this young man appeared so hostile. She'd never met him before. As Professor Faber's assistant, she expected him to at least be polite, if not friendly. She always thought the best of people until proven otherwise, but he seemed to think people were suspect until proven otherwise.

"Since you're in town, you should join the tour. Each house has its own story." Maggie reached under the counter and brought out a flyer. "Here, take this. It's a list of the buildings with their descriptions and a map." She held it out to him.

Conrad took the paper, laid it on the counter, and studied it. "I've looked around the antiques shop already." He turned the map over and pointed to the description of Sedgwick Manor. "I'm looking forward to going inside your house." He stressed the word *inside*.

"You'll find it's quite beautiful. A lot of thought and care went into details like the woodwork, doors, and stairs." Maggie slipped into the friendly instructional cadence she used when talking to tourists. "The workers were incredibly skillful, and the house shines with their craftsmanship."

"I'm sure. I'm also quite interested in how it's furnished, its decor, that sort of thing."

Maggie wondered at his comment. He didn't strike her as the sort who was drawn to fine antiques. But then, it wasn't as if he'd been overly conversational about such things.

"The house is much as my aunt Evelyn left it. If you like eighteenth- and nineteenth-century furnishings, you'll enjoy it."

Conrad picked up the flyer. "Didn't you bring any of your own stuff with you? Perhaps some First American art from your husband's collection?"

Maggie couldn't help but feel he was implying something was wrong if she did have such artifacts on display. Was he suggesting she was one of those unscrupulous collectors he had mentioned when he first met her? But when she looked into his eyes, they reflected an innocent curiosity, not an accusation.

"No. We never collected. As you said, most archaeologists don't."

Conrad folded the flyer and put it in his back pocket. "I'll see you tonight."

As she watched him leave the building, Maggie couldn't decide if that was a promise or a threat.

8

It was midafternoon by the time Maggie and June found time for a breather at the counter. Through the shop windows, they watched rain clouds move over the town.

"I hope it doesn't rain," June said. "It will discourage people from turning out tonight." As if to distract herself from the threat of bad weather, she swiveled around on her chair to face Maggie and began to regale her with stories of the morning's customers.

"Those young ones were fascinated by the idea of having a pirate's bedroom," June said. "I heard them telling their parents that they wanted a bedroom just like ours." She sat back. "The parents solved that one by telling them they could have one of those porthole mirrors and perhaps even a treasure chest."

"Maybe we should ferret out more old chests," Maggie said. "I think I know where we can get a few more porthole frames too. A customer from Portland said her family had some from her grandfather's old boat and asked me if I'd be interested in them."

"Great idea. They are definitely going to be popular items. Not everyone can use a whole bedroom set, but a few smaller items would develop a similar theme for their children."

Soon, the party furniture arrived and was quickly set up by the deliverymen. Maggie had ordered long rectangular banquet tables to hold refreshments and tall cocktail tables for people to stand around while enjoying their snacks and drinks.

A delivery from The Singing Mermaid turned up around four o'clock. June cast an appreciative eye on the bouquets. "Thank goodness for florists," she said, grinning. "Not much is blooming just now, but here we have all the spring flowers we need."

Maggie nodded in agreement. The bouquets did look lovely. Larger vases of daffodils and tulips were placed strategically on the rectangular food and drink tables. Bunches of delicate crocus and Star of Bethlehem in glass containers tied with colorful ribbons were placed on the tall round tables.

The Graham twins showed up a little later than expected with the food. While Maggie appreciated their delicious delicacies, their work style verged on chaotic, causing her to wonder if things would actually be ready in time. However, once there, the twins worked quickly and efficiently. They had hired a couple of extra helpers to carry and distribute the refreshments between the carriage house and the manor.

To Maggie's immense relief, everything was ready by six o'clock, giving her time for a refreshing shower. She dressed in black and added a lustrous, single-strand pearl necklace. She swept her hair up and back, holding it in place with an antique cloisonné comb.

Snickers would be closed in her bedroom for the evening, so she made sure he had his litter box, food, and water. "Sorry, buddy. I'll make it up to you later." She gave him a short, affectionate rub under his chin and then, as he sat watching her, closed the door on her way out.

James, who was planning to begin and end the evening at the manor with periodic check-ins at other tour sites, was the first to arrive. His perfectly fitted blue suit accented his eyes, which sparkled in the glow of the candles lit in the foyer. Maggie suddenly felt a rush of shyness.

"You look lovely," he said.

"You do too," she answered, then laughed at the expression on his face when she called him "lovely." He chuckled too, his voice mingling easily with hers.

Eric, who wore dark pants with a white shirt and tie, followed directly behind James.

"Looking good, pal," James said, giving him a light tap on the shoulder.

"You do look sharp, Eric," Maggie said in agreement before getting down to business. "As I mentioned earlier, I'd like you to keep watch for any candles that blow out, any napkins and cups that don't make it into the garbage, things like that. Sound good?"

"Sure thing, boss," Eric said.

The evening whirled by in a blur of greetings, brief tours, and discussions of antiques. There was a constant flow of townspeople and early seasonal tourists. The rooms of Sedgwick Manor glowed in the soft candlelight as people milled about, relishing the twins' food and a cup of something warm to drink.

Fortunately, the weather had cooperated. The earlier impending rain never fell, although clouds blocked any light the quarter moon might have lent them, and the temperature retained a reasonable spring coolness.

As Maggie walked around, mingling with the ever-changing flow of people, she spotted a few who had passed through her shop earlier in the week. The mother-daughter duo chatted amicably with the couple from Boston and a man in a tan jacket she thought could be the mint man. As she studied him, the man reached toward a platter of Needhams and faced her. She recognized him instead as the fellow from South Carolina who had been in the shop a couple of times with his wife.

Soon Maggie spotted Conrad examining her tiger oak bowfront china cabinets, dating from the late 1800s. The subdued lighting left the cabinets' interiors a bit dark, making it difficult to fully appreciate their contents. Conrad was hunched over, bending close to peer inside.

"My aunt and I shared a love of porcelain," Maggie said,

coming up beside him. "Some of those pieces are from China."

"They look quite delicate. I understand that if a cup is good porcelain, you can see through it."

She laughed. "Only bone china, and it's not like looking through glass. You can see shadows, but that's about it. Bone china is so strong that a cup or plate can be thin enough to let light through. Its name and its strength come from animal bone ash, which is added to it before it's fired."

"That bowl seems to have a lot of cracks. I suppose that's because of some mistake in the firing," he said pointing at a shallow bowl.

"That's celadon from the Northern Song Dynasty, around AD 960 to 1127. It's called Yaozhou ware. The cracks are a distinctive part of the pottery. It's how they achieved contrast to give their pieces more detail."

Conrad widened his eyes in apparent surprise at her detailed knowledge and description.

"I read it in Aunt Evelyn's journal," she admitted. "She loved beautiful antiques and had eclectic taste, so she collected a bit of everything. Besides, Chinese pottery was somewhat popular in the 1800s among the more well-to-do and was found in the best Maine homes. You'll find chinaware in most of the larger antiques shops in the area and even in some of the smaller ones."

"It dates to around the time of the Anasazi," Conrad said. He moved to the other side of the cabinet where there were three vases. "These are so bright." He pointed to a pair of blue-on-white vases.

"That white background color is another of porcelain's distinctive features. You really can't get that dazzling white with other types of pottery."

Conrad bent even closer to the cabinet's window, inspecting the pieces. Then he straightened up and stepped back. With his eyes still on the contents, he said, "Yeah, the Anasazi pottery is beautiful, but because of its clay, the sides have to be a lot thicker than this. I haven't studied Chinese pottery, but I might need to. This is stunning."

His admiration for the early Chinese technology and skill was evident. Maggie smiled. He spoke like a true archaeologist.

Conrad looked through the second bowfront cabinet, then stood and thrust his hands into his pockets. "I don't see any First American pieces. Where do you keep those?" His eyes searched the room.

Maggie stepped back. "I already told you, I don't have any." She gave him a hard look. "I have to see to my other guests. The refreshment table is over there. Why don't you go help yourself?" With that, she left.

Watching people explore her home and converse animatedly about this and that lifted Maggie's spirits. After a long winter, this evening's festivities seemed to be just what everyone needed. Throughout the rooms, groups of guests laughed and shared stories about their families' ties to the town and community.

Maggie overheard many folks mention that the brown paper bags with flickering candles lighting the path between the manor and the antiques shop added a romantic touch. She smiled. It had been June's idea, and a great one at that. She would make sure to tell June how much people loved it.

Before Maggie knew it, nine thirty came. As the clock struck the half hour, the remaining visitors seemed sorry to see the evening end and slowly took their leave. Several suggested on the way out that future tours should go later into the evening. She made a mental note to pass this suggestion on to James.

Once the last person had departed, the rental service and the twins' crew had everything dismantled and cleaned away in record time. Maggie let Eric go home, and she and James went over to the shop to help June lock up. Here, too, the crews had already finished their cleanup job.

"I saw your cranky friend tonight," June said as they watched the twins' team take the last trays out the door.

"My cranky friend?" Maggie asked.

"Conrad, that professor's assistant."

"Oh, I'm surprised that he came over. He said he had seen the antiques shop and made it sound like he was only going to come to the manor."

"Maybe he wanted to eat more and didn't want to take too much from one place," James said jokingly.

"I don't get the impression that he's the type to care what anyone would think about what he ate or didn't eat," Maggie said.

James studied her face. "This fellow bothers you, doesn't he?"

She looked from James to June. "I know it's silly, but I always feel like he's accusing me of a crime, and I don't have a clue what it is. I've never seen this guy before, but he just doesn't seem to like me."

"It could simply be his personality," June said. "He may not even realize he appears so disagreeable to others."

"Who is he anyway?" James wanted to know.

Maggie and June quickly filled him in.

"Maybe he's disgruntled because he expected to pick up a bunch of boxes and be back home by now," James said.

"Perhaps." Maggie scrunched her mouth and decided to put Conrad out of her mind. She'd see him again soon enough, she was sure.

Casting a tired eye at the crumbs and other debris on the floor, Maggie said, "This can be taken care of tomorrow. You should go home, June."

June nodded, rubbed her back, and slipped on her coat before heading out while Maggie locked up the building.

Watching June's SUV leave the parking lot, James said, "I'll walk you back to the house."

Maggie and James slowly moved along the path, making sure

each luminary was extinguished. The darkness filled in behind them, the crunch of stones under their feet the only sound.

As they strolled along together, they revisited the evening. They discussed the possibility of doing it again next year, and if they did, what they might change. Maggie enjoyed sharing her ideas with James, and he was an attentive listener. By the time they'd reached the house, they had agreed to get together the next day at The Busy Bean to continue their conversation.

After James left, Maggie double-checked the windows and doors, got ready for bed, and crawled under the covers. Preparing for tonight had taken a lot of planning and work, but it had been worth it. She pulled the blankets up to her chin and sighed contentedly.

Snickers sat at the bedside, meowing insistently.

She turned toward him. "And good night to you too."

He went to the window and jumped onto the sill to look out into the night, still meowing.

"Now what are you up to? Not happy because you had to stay in the room? I'm sorry, but it was for your own good. Everything's back to normal now, so don't fret." She lay back down and bade him another sleepy good night.

The last thing she saw before she succumbed to deep sleep was Snickers, still at the window, peering into the darkness.

9

An incessant buzzing woke Maggie from a deep, exhausted sleep. Groggily, she looked around her darkened room. Her cell phone lit up as it vibrated, quit, then vibrated again. Her bedside clock read two o'clock in the morning.

Who could be calling at this time? She reached out for the phone, bracing herself for bad news.

"Maggie, it's Harry Carter. Daisy's husband," he added, as if she might not remember him in her groggy haze.

"Harry? Is Daisy okay?"

"She's fine. But I'm sitting in my truck across from your shop, and I think someone broke in. A light keeps appearing in different windows, like someone is looking around with a flashlight."

At first, his words didn't make sense, but when he said "broke in," Maggie suddenly jolted awake.

"What're you doing out there?" she asked, sitting up.

Harry expelled a frustrated puff of air. "I had to work late on one of my lobster boats. Engine timing was off. Beginning of the season and lots to set up, that kind of thing. Anyway, when I was driving past your shop, I noticed a light moving from window to window."

Taking in what he said, Maggie threw off the covers and flung her legs over the side of the bed. "Don't go in there, Harry. I'm calling the police."

"I already called them. I'll keep an eye on it in case the guy comes out before the police arrive."

"But only to identify him. Don't do anything rash." She threw on workout clothes, then grabbed her phone, the keys to the shop, and her new flashlight from Ina.

Maggie knew the police would arrive soon, but a surge of impatience and outrage at the invasion of her property made her dash out the door and head toward the carriage house.

The ample arms of the trees lining the path created large, inky patches in the already-dark path running between the buildings. Having used the walkway so many times, Maggie could have traversed it blindfolded. Now she ran headlong toward the black tunnel, rushing to the shop. As she approached it, however, she slowed down, then stopped. A breeze blew through the trees, and the soft squeaking of one branch rubbing on another filled the silence.

She looked at the street. Harry's truck was parked at the curb, its interior lost in a blanket of black. She couldn't see him, but she was glad he was there.

Maggie stepped toward the shop's entrance, moving carefully along the building's side and remaining in the deep shadow of its eaves.

The loud bang of a door being slammed drew her attention to the back of the shop. She froze, searching through the blackness for the noise's source.

A figure, merely a darker form against the world's darkness, ran from the shop and was swallowed by the night. She clicked the flashlight on and pointed it in the runner's direction, but the person had already disappeared into the vegetation. She started to follow, but intense flashing blue lights and a siren announced the police's arrival. Officer Clayton, once again on night shift, burst from the squad car.

Maggie turned on her flashlight and shined it in the officer's direction. "Over here!" she called. "I saw someone run this way." She pointed the flashlight beam into the yard, creating a passage of light through the darkness.

The officer looked askance at Maggie as she passed with her

own powerful flashlight, her face making it clear she didn't approve of her presence.

Nevertheless, without a word, Officer Clayton started after the culprit, Maggie keeping pace just behind her. Their flashlights swung arcs of light through the yard and trees, but they had lost track of the thief.

They returned to the front of the carriage house. Maggie angled her light toward Harry's truck but didn't see him. It appeared that only an empty pickup remained parked across the street, parallel parked between two other cars. "I wonder what happened to Harry."

"He probably went after that thief too," Officer Clayton said.

Maggie shivered in the night air. "He'll be back soon."

"I hope he can ID the intruder," Officer Clayton said. "He was already too far gone for me to get a look." She glanced over at Maggie. "What did you see?"

Maggie shook her head. "Nothing much. It was too dark. All I saw was a figure running. I don't even know if it was a man or woman." She ran her hand through her hair, pushing it behind her ears.

"Let's check inside and see what was taken," Officer Clayton said. "I'll also look for anything that might help us figure out who did this."

They walked through the store, doing a quick survey. The debris from the evening's tour was still scattered about on the floor: crumbs, a few pieces of candy, crumpled napkins. Maggie picked up the napkins and candy, depositing them in a small trash bin behind the counter.

Everything looked normal. With such a cursory check, Maggie couldn't be sure if anything was stolen. In the morning, June would have to also look through the shop for missing merchandise. After that, they could clean up from the tour traffic. Glancing at the messy floor, Maggie thought about all of the people who had come though this evening, most eating and drinking. She scowled at the debris. It would be difficult, if not impossible, for the police to determine what was from the party and what might be clues left behind by the thief.

Maggie examined the back storeroom. The door was open, a sign the intruder had been there. Yet again, apparently nothing was taken. There were no other telltale signs that she could discern. She bit her lower lip in consternation. There had to be clues. Was she simply missing them? No one could come and go without leaving any trace.

"I don't get it," Maggie said to Officer Clayton. "Nothing seems to be missing. The guy ran away before I got here. I didn't have my flashlight or my phone on. How did he know I was coming?"

The officer, who was checking the windows for signs of forced entry, shook her head.

Maggie sighed. "Maybe we'll know more when Harry gets back."

While Officer Clayton finished her own search, Maggie inspected the cash register for signs of tampering but found none. After digging her shop keys out of her pocket, Maggie unlocked the cash register drawer and checked inside. Nothing was missing.

"I'm going up to the attic for a final check," the officer said over her shoulder as she started up the stairs.

"The attic's locked," Maggie said. "The thief wouldn't be able to get in there."

"I'll check to be sure it's secure, just to be thorough."

Maggie nodded and turned back to the counter, vaguely aware of the stomping of the policewoman's heavy boots as she rapidly climbed the steps. Maggie stood staring at the register, lost in thought.

She heard the officer coming back down. But Officer Clayton's boots thumped differently this time. Each footstep was followed by another, longer *thrump*. Maggie glanced over at the stairs. Officer Clayton staggered into view with an injured Harry Carter.

Harry's head was covered in blood.

10

Officer Clayton dragged Harry as much as she helped him walk. Once they reached the counter, she eased him into a chair. His hand trembling, Harry gingerly held a handkerchief to his forehead. Red splotches grew in an expanding circle on the white cloth.

Maggie rushed around the counter. "What happened?"

"I found Harry sprawled out on the floor upstairs in the attic," Officer Clayton said. "The door was wide open. Apparently, the thief was inside and heard Harry coming. They knocked him out and ran."

"Harry." Maggie almost groaned as she stared at his battered face. "I told you to stay in the truck."

He looked up at her, a guilty look in his eyes. "I couldn't let some thieving monster come in here and steal from you. What kind of man would I be?"

"A man without a head injury," Officer Clayton answered grimly. "Not to mention the fact that if you'd stayed in your truck instead of going after the guy, he might still have been here when I arrived." Pivoting to Maggie, she went on matter-of-factly, "Harry'll be okay. Heads bleed easily. He could use a bandage, though. Do you have a first aid kit here?"

"Let's go over to the house," she said. "There's a kit in the bathroom." Whatever was—or wasn't—in the attic could wait.

* * *

Once Harry was looked after, the three sat down in Maggie's

living room. Officer Clayton took notes on what each had witnessed.

"I saw that moving light," Harry said. "Called the police, then Maggie. When I got to the store, the front door was cracked open, so I stepped in quietly. I heard someone upstairs, so I went up. Those confounded old steps squeaked, and he heard me coming. I could have got him if it weren't for those stairs."

Perched on the edge of her chair, Maggie wondered if she noted a smirk on Officer Clayton's lips at this declaration.

"He was waiting for you at the top?" the policewoman asked.

"The attic door was wide open. It was black as a raven's wings inside. No light. As I told Maggie, he must have only used a flashlight. Couldn't very well turn on a light, could he?" Harry scowled. "I'd hoped he hadn't heard me coming, but when I stuck my head in the door, he must have whopped me, because that's all I remember 'til you came, Samantha."

"Were you able to see who it was?"

"Only wish I could have," Harry replied. "Never saw anything. Except stars."

Maggie wasn't able to add anything of use. She suspected this strange break-in had something to do with the Anasazi pots tucked away in the attic, but she had no proof, nothing beyond her suspicions. The would-be thief could have been rummaging through the store and, finding the locked door, thought something of greater value than what was displayed below had to be behind it. *I suppose that's technically true.*

"Thank you both," Officer Clayton said, putting her notebook away once they'd completed telling her whatever they could. "I'll be making out a report on the break-in. Unfortunately, from what you two could tell me, there may not be much we can do." An almost-apologetic look passed over her features as she rolled her pen between her fingers. "After my search just now I didn't find any indication of the thief's identity or even what he or she wanted."

"It is quite the mystery," Maggie said.

Officer Clayton pursed her lips. "Once again, the perpetrator apparently got in through a back window that had been left unlocked or even open."

Maggie's head popped up and she gripped the arm of her chair. "I'm sure I closed and locked every window. I checked before the party." She racked her brain, trying to remember what she, James, and June had done. Then she shook her head. "But I don't think James, June, or I checked the windows again after the tour was over."

Harry chimed in. "So someone could have opened a window during the tour?"

Maggie nodded weakly. "The evening went well. We had a much bigger crowd than we'd even hoped for. As far as we know there were no mishaps. Everyone seemed to have a good time. By the time it was over, we were so tired that we just locked up as usual."

"If that's the case, then it's possible that the perp entered the shop during the tour along with the other guests and unlocked the window, expecting to come back later," Officer Clayton said.

Snickers, who had been scarce, came sauntering into the room and brushed against the police officer's leg.

"How are you doing, big fella?" she said and leaned down to caress his back and scratch around his head and chin. He flopped over onto his back and let her pet his white tummy.

Everyone laughed at Snickers's antics, breaking the night's tension. Maggie's sense of being personally invaded by the would-be thief lessened. She leaned back against the chair's cushion and laid her arm along its carved armrest.

A short while later, Officer Clayton delivered another brief sermon about being careful and locking up. "And remember," she said, giving Maggie and Harry stern looks as she prepared to leave, "when you call 911, you aren't supposed to run after the culprit. Leave that to the police." Then she scratched Snickers on his head one more time and headed out the door.

Harry followed her into the night.

Alone, Maggie went over the events of the past few days. Someone had tried to break into both Sedgwick Manor and the antiques store, but nothing was taken either time. Was the intruder in each case the same person? Were they unrelated, coincidental events? It was the beginning of tourist season. New people in town. If these were random crimes, it was especially strange that nothing had been taken in either case. Could the intruder be searching for something he hadn't found—yet?

Frustrated by the break-ins, Maggie mulled over her situation. The question "Would he try again?" kept popping up in her mind. Nevertheless, she remained resistant to the idea of burglar alarms. Ina had given her that heavy flashlight with its intense beam because it was advertised as a safe defense against a night attack. Maggie began to slip it back into the kitchen drawer, then stopped. She'd keep it on her bedside table instead. Just in case.

Her thoughts turned toward her aunt, as they often did. Aunt Evelyn had lived in this house her whole adult life. Much of the time she lived alone. Obviously, from what Maggie knew, Evelyn had never felt the need for an alarm system. This was her town, her home. She was comfortable in it. Not careless, but secure nonetheless.

As Maggie mulled over the security issues, the image of a feisty Ina volunteering to help her came to mind and cinched her decision to not let a petty thief disturb her life. She only hoped she had the spirit that Ina had when she reached those years of her life.

Maggie drew in a deep breath and let it out. She felt better.

She went into the living room to turn off the lights for the night. Snickers sat in the middle of the Turkish rug, watching her. As she crossed the room, her foot ran into something soft. She bent over to see what it was and found a catnip-filled toy mouse. She picked it up and tossed it into the middle of the floor.

At first, Snickers stared at it without moving. Then, he slowly crouched down and froze, gaze still fixed on his target. Without warning, he pounced.

In the dim room, Maggie sat back in a wingback chair, watching her tabby play with the mouse as if it were a ferocious live enemy instead of just a toy. He stalked it, then pounced again, seizing it in a tight hold with his sharp teeth.

Maggie continued to contemplate recent events, unsettled by the feeling that cat-and-mouse games weren't just for Snickers.

11

By late morning the next day, Eric hadn't come in to work.

"Is he beginning to make a habit of not coming in to work on time?" June wondered out loud. "And without even a call to let us know? We don't have much going on today, but what if we had a delivery and had been counting on him?"

Maggie frowned. A thought worse than unreliability grew in her mind. She stared out the window at the ominous gray clouds signaling an impending storm. What if his absence was due to last night's break-in? Could he have been the shadowy figure she saw running from the building?

She passed a hand over her eyes, fighting the image of bright, enthusiastic Eric being their thief.

June's voice took on a more conciliatory tone. "Of course, he might have had to do something for his dad and simply forgot. And he did tell us he's been pretty stressed about starting back at school after so long."

"Ah, yes," Maggie said. "That's probably it."

Maggie pulled out her phone and called Eric. No answer. She left a short voice mail asking him to call the shop. Next, thinking he might be at an appointment with his dad and had his phone turned off, she typed a text message also requesting that he get in touch with her.

"Well, we'll know what happened eventually," June said once Maggie put her phone back into her pocket. "In the meantime, I need to check on that new inventory we received." She stepped toward the storage room, clipboard in hand.

Taking over the main desk, Maggie turned on the computer. Once the screen lit up and she'd opened a browser window, she typed in *Southern Maine Community College*. She pulled up the social sciences department and their course offerings for the current semester. Names like *Introduction to Anthropology* and *Introduction to Physical Anthropology* were listed, but nothing on Native Americans or on anything resembling that topic came up.

Maggie sat back and gazed at the college's list of classes bracketed by photos of smiling students. *Is Eric lying about taking a course on First Americans? Why would he do such a thing?*

She chewed the inside of her cheek in consternation. Images of Richard's archaeological materials in the carriage house attic and the loose tape on one of the boxes popped into her mind. Eric knew about all of the boxes up there and, as an employee, he had access to the attic. He knew about First American artifacts and their value, and his father was racking up medical bills.

Maggie's heart was heavy as she exited from the college's website.

June came back, clipboard in hand. "Everything seems to be in place and okay. Now I'll go through the rest of the shop."

When she returned, declaring everything seemed in order, they sat and discussed the situation. It was baffling—nothing appeared to be missing. Their locked cash register hadn't been tampered with either.

As they replayed the events from the past few days, a quick-stepping, white-haired woman blew into the shop as if by a strong gust of wind.

"I heard that you had a second break-in last night," Ina announced, pulling the door shut behind her. "The police scan reported it about two o'clock. Is that right? A second one? Oh, Maggie."

"It's okay, Ina," Maggie said quickly. "Nothing was stolen.

Apparently, we interrupted the thief before he could take anything."

"After he attacked poor Harry," Ina said angrily.

Maggie nodded. "That was terrible. He was hit on the head, but he will be okay. After a little TLC last night, he drove himself home. Officer Clayton did a thorough investigation."

"With no results," Ina said.

Boy, those police scanners are almost as good as the local gossip mill. Ina always seemed strong and capable, full of energy and ready to dive into any project, but Maggie still didn't want her friend to become excited or upset over attempted thefts. Fortunately, she needn't have worried.

"Samantha and the rest of our police force are good at their jobs," Ina said. "They'll get to the bottom of this, I'm sure." Her bright eyes took in Maggie and June. "You already know you should be watchful, but remember: It's only property. It's not worth getting hurt over."

Relieved that Ina was instructing them to be careful and not stewing about things, Maggie nodded. Soon June had diverted Ina's attention from the crimes by asking her about the history behind some new pieces they had in the shop. Ina was a font of local historical knowledge. Maggie watched as the two wandered the aisles, with June asking questions and Ina cheerfully delving into the personal or local historical stories behind a piece of furniture or a picture.

Ina's voice drifted over to Maggie as they stopped at a large walnut frame with an oval convex glass. "Oh, I remember this being in Tammy Larson's house in the '50s. It's an early photograph of her . . ."

By the time Ina left the shop, Maggie was certain that, although the diminutive historian remained concerned, she was no longer overly troubled by the incidents.

The shop had settled into its normal daily activities by noon, when James called to invite Maggie for lunch at The Busy Bean. She was delighted, both because she enjoyed spending time with James and also because she wanted to talk with Daisy and check up on Harry. Maggie had reassured Ina that Harry was fine, but now she wanted further proof herself.

She was pretty sure Harry would never admit to suffering from last night's run-in, no matter how he truly felt. As his wife, Daisy was able to read him better than he could read himself, and Maggie knew she would level with her about how well Harry was actually doing. June assured Maggie that she was fine on her own and would let her know when Eric came in—if he came in.

Maggie had barely stepped inside The Busy Bean when Daisy—wearing an A-line dress covered in a large, bright paisley print and cinched at the waist—made a beeline for her. Before Daisy reached her, James waved at her from a spot by the window. She caught Daisy's arm and pulled her to the table, where she tucked herself into a seat across from James.

Daisy put her order pad down and stood close to them. Without pausing, she blurted out what she knew of the attempted break-in from Harry's version of the story, which Maggie already knew for the most part. Finishing, she said, "Now, what have you got to say, Maggie? What did Officer Clayton's investigation turn up? What did you and June find? What was stolen?"

Her questions piled up on one another and Maggie was sure nearby tables heard every word: Daisy's entire rendition, given in high drama for effect, and her list of questions.

Once Daisy was done, Maggie made sure Harry was indeed on the mend, then said in a gentler, much more conversational tone, "I am so thankful Harry saw lights on his way home and called. It was fortunate for me that he happened to be working late. If he hadn't been, who knows what the thief might have stolen? Normally, it's rare for anyone to be up and around at that time of night."

Daisy gave a knowing look. "Yeah, a town like ours usually rolls up the sidewalk and everyone goes home to bed after the stores close."

"Precisely," Maggie said. "I called the police immediately. Officer Clayton was at the shop within minutes."

"You should have called me too," James said, his brow furrowed.

Maggie studied his face and then looked up at Daisy. She was touched by their obvious worry for her.

"It all turned out okay. Really, the police are on top of it."

"Does your daughter know about this?" Daisy asked.

Maggie felt a pang. "No, and I don't want her to know. There's nothing she can do, and worrying will interfere with her studies."

"You're right," James said. "She doesn't have to be told every detail right now. You can fill her in later when this is all behind us."

Maggie gave him a small smile of gratitude. She appreciated his support in her choice not to tell Emily just yet. She knew she was making the right decision, but it was good to hear someone else confirm it.

Apparently satisfied that she'd learned all she could, Daisy took Maggie's and James's orders and went to the kitchen.

Speaking in a barely audible voice, Maggie leaned over the table toward James. "There's something that is bothering me, though." She cast a quick glance around at the tables near them. She didn't want anyone else to hear. "It's about Eric."

James raised his eyebrows in a question. "What about him?"

She went on. "He's been behaving rather oddly lately."

"What do you mean?"

"Well, at first he was reliable and conscientious about being to work on time and doing his assigned tasks. Not one problem.

But the other day he came in late, saying he couldn't sleep and was studying for an exam. This morning he didn't come in at all. I just don't know what to make of it."

James studied her. "Getting back into the challenge of reading texts, memorizing bits of information, and even writing papers can be daunting at first. Why does that trouble you? Do you think it's interfering with his ability to work?"

She shook her head. "It's not that. He said he's taking a First Americans class, but I checked the community college's course offerings this morning. A First Americans class isn't being taught this semester. He lied to me."

"I'm sorry, Maggie."

"He seems so nice. I really like him. His eagerness reminds me of some of Richard's favorite students." Doubt clouded her eyes as she looked out the window. "Now I'm wondering if he isn't *too* interested."

"Too interested in what?" James asked.

She brought her gaze back to his handsome face. "Once he learned that I have a few boxes of Richard's archaeological materials and artifacts, he started talking incessantly about them."

"Okay, I can see how you might think that's a problem. But he's an enthusiastic guy. Maybe he's not expressing himself very well about it. Everyone needs a passion. My mother's is quilting, mine is restoring antiques. It's healthy and normal."

"Yes, but he also seems to be particularly interested in their value. When June asked him what he would do if he had a valuable First American artifact, he immediately said he'd sell it. Now I'm wondering if it isn't just about the money that this pottery would bring." Maggie grimaced.

James tapped his fingers on the table. "You're wondering if there's a connection between his interests and the mysterious break-ins."

Maggie, miserable at hearing it actually stated out loud, nodded. "Still, I don't want to jump to conclusions. Nothing's been taken, so I don't know for sure that the thief was after Richard's antiquities. And there's nothing to identify the person. It could be a woman or a man. It could be someone who's older or younger. We don't know anything. It's just that . . ."

"It's just that these coincidences are beginning to look like a pattern. And Eric fits into the pattern."

"Well, yeah. There's no way around it."

Just then, the door to the café opened. The Graham twins entered, bearing large trays. Bright smiles lit up their faces. Seeing Maggie with James, they came over to their table first.

"Daisy plans to sell some of our desserts," Francine said excitedly. She swept a hand in front of her tray, indicating an assortment of baked goods. "These are all fresh this morning."

Maggie eyed the trays. Needhams and whoopie pies, each wrapped in cellophane and tied with a ribbon, were artfully displayed. "You must have been up since dawn making all those," she said.

Francine nodded, fairly dancing with delight. "This will be huge for our business and will give us a steady income while we get established in our catering too. Everyone comes to the café, locals and tourists. This is the best advertisement ever."

"Here's a copy of our newest flyer," Lydia said, offering Maggie and James a brightly colored trifold brochure. On its front, under *The Maine Occasion*, was a drawing of a motherlike figure baking in a cozy kitchen.

"We had those made up this morning too," Francine said. "Aren't they great?"

"I'd be happy to carry these in my shop," Maggie offered. "We have a display that holds advertisements from local businesses."

Francine squealed. "Oh, would you?"

Lydia shot an embarrassed glance at her sister but gave a lopsided grin.

Pleased with their reaction, Maggie said, "Drop by anytime this afternoon. June is there. She'll show you where to put them."

"We'll do that," Francine said. "And we'll leave something special for you too."

When the girls moved to the next table, James said, "That was good of you. It's important for all of us in the community to support one another. We're not like the big cities. There, competition is more important. Here, we're in one boat and we survive or not as one."

Maggie admired Somerset Harbor's sense of community, that wanting to support and protect each other. That commitment seemed so strong here, in the small coastal Maine towns, and she was happy to be part of it.

Before leaving the café, Maggie checked her text messages. She had texts from both Eric and June. Eric had sent a message apologizing, saying he hadn't thought he was scheduled to work that day and was studying instead. He promised to be in later. June's text was the same. Maggie sighed and sent a brief *Okay* back to both.

As she left The Busy Bean, however, a couple down the block and across the street caught her eye. They strolled along, heads close together, sharing a joke. She stopped and stared after them as they turned the corner.

The young man was Eric, and she was sure the girl was Connie.

12

"Are you the manager?"

Maggie looked up and into hazel eyes encircled by a pair of red glasses. The woman placed a large, embroidered felt handbag on the counter and pushed back wisps of gray hair.

"I'm the owner. May I help you?"

"I'm Mrs. Baranowski," she said, straightening the sleeves of her houndstooth jacket and pulling them down to her wrists, covering her gray turtleneck sweater's sleeve. "I recently moved to a small place on South Doe Island. I suppose you know it?"

"I visited South Doe Island once when I was a child," Maggie said. "But I haven't had a chance to go again. I've heard it's quite beautiful."

The woman smiled. "That's why I chose it. Beautiful and peaceful. I was a schoolteacher in New Jersey and have lived in a city for most of my life. Don't get me wrong. It was a good life. But now that I'm retired, I want to live surrounded by the beauty and quiet of nature."

"South Doe Island should have plenty of both. Is there something you were looking for?"

"Well, I noticed you were selling a large chest back in that bedroom area." Mrs. Baranowski paused.

"Are you interested in looking at it more closely?" Maggie asked.

"No. Not because it's not beautiful, but because my new home is . . . cozy." She grinned. "Quite cozy. One of those 'tiny house' things, and there's no storage space left. I find that I no longer have room for even some of the few pieces I brought with me, including my collection of chests. Each one is distinctive and would be a lovely addition to almost any decor." She sighed. "Downsizing was quite difficult and—even though I was able to part with a good many of my things—I overestimated how much I could keep. As a result, my garage is full. But now that I'm coming to terms with what making a lifestyle change means, I think I'm ready to part with more of my belongings, including several trunks much like the one you have on display."

As the woman went on describing the items she would be willing to sell, the front door opened. Along with a blast of cold air, Conrad entered the shop. He caught Maggie glancing over at him, and offered a smug smile and curt bob of the head as a greeting.

It's only Saturday. Why is he here? Did he think I meant I'd give him the boxes immediately after the History by Candlelight Tour was over?

Maggie took a deep breath. He was an outsider, so he probably hadn't heard about the break-in at the antiques shop. It was something everyone in town knew about. They didn't need a radio announcement or an article in the paper.

He sauntered up to the counter. "So are you ready now?"

Mrs. Baranowski, startled by his rudeness, stopped talking and gaped at him.

Maggie tried not to glare as she said, "I thought I told you things would be ready for you to take back later in the week. Not now. Not today."

Conrad merely looked at her.

Realizing her annoyance showed, she softened her tone. "I'm sorry Professor Faber told you to come so early and that you have to wait around so long, but it can't be helped. We've been terribly busy. I believe I can have everything ready by the end of next week." She wouldn't let Conrad's arrival interrupt her business.

His eyes flitted briefly over Mrs. Baranowski. "No problem," he said with a smirk, then meandered away. He stopped at the nearest display case, which was filled with silver and gold necklaces along with a collection of antique white-gold diamond rings. He began studying them as if they held the secrets of the universe.

"I believe they are all antiques," Mrs. Baranowski went on.

"I'm sorry, what?" Maggie shook her head as though clearing her mind.

"My trunks, dear. I don't know exactly how old they are. I've had them for forty or more years myself, and I bought them all at antiques shops like yours." The older woman looked around the room. "I wonder if you'd be interested in selling them through consignment or maybe purchasing them outright." She shuffled through her purse and pulled out a mobile phone. "I have some pictures, if you'd care to see them," she said, holding the phone out for Maggie to see.

Maggie studied a picture of two piles of chests stacked on each other. Each was partially covered by a rug. The rugs protected the chests' surfaces from being scratched or gouged by the chest stacked on its top. Even though it was difficult to determine their exact quality, they did appear to be worth further investigation.

"Well, before I make any decisions, I'd have to actually see the chests," Maggie said. She was thrilled at the possibility of getting more trunks. Already, several customers had inquired about buying the pirate chest in the display. However, she hadn't wanted to sell it before the tour. It was a critical part of the scene's playful ambiance.

"Ah, well, you see, that may be a problem." Mrs. Baranowski grimaced. "I don't have an easy way to get them over to the mainland."

"I understand." Maggie glanced at her full calendar, already anticipating the next question.

"I don't suppose you could come over to South Doe Island?

It's too early in the season for the tourist boats, but the mail boat runs twice a day, once in the morning and again in midafternoon."

Maggie considered. If the chests were of good quality, this could be a very timely opportunity for her business. She'd take Eric along to help bring the chests back. *As long as he remembers to turn up for work.*

"How does Monday sound? I need to make sure my assistant is available, though. Can I call you later to confirm?"

Mrs. Baranowski's eyes lit up. "Perfect. And I'll show you around when you're there."

As soon as the older woman stepped away from the counter, Conrad approached.

"I was passing by and thought it'd be a good time to stop in and find out when I can pick up Professor Faber's research materials," he said.

It was all Maggie could do to keep from showing her exasperation with him. Then she thought about his being here in Somerset Harbor, just waiting to do what his professor had asked him to do. It wasn't her fault Faber told him to come too early, but that didn't matter. He was here. He probably had work to do at home and hated waiting, doing nothing for days. She glanced at his big hand resting on the counter. It was calloused. He was used to being in the field or in the lab, not stuck in a small town because someone else's lines had gotten crossed. His edginess and continued impatience told her that.

Maggie reviewed the calendar she had laid out on the counter. "You'll be glad to know that I will be able to go through everything and put aside Professor Faber's materials by the end of this week." She looked up at him, her finger resting on next Saturday's date.

He frowned. "Next Saturday?" He was about to say

something but then looked away briefly before continuing. "Faber said you're busy. That's why he wanted me to come. I know what to look for. I can complete the task of finding those containers in no time."

She cocked her head. "What do they look like? How would you know which ones are his without looking through all the boxes?"

He grinned, and it was one of his rare, honest smiles. "Every one is in a heavy-duty cardboard box marked with a large black *SW* on the side. It stands for *Southwest*, as in Southwestern Native Americans."

He'd just described the boxes Maggie had been worrying over and wondering why they were originally sent to Richard and why he'd never mentioned them to her. They seemed to carry a secret, a secret she wanted, needed, to know. A secret involving her husband.

"They're easy to spot," Conrad continued. "Just let me do it. You don't have to make it difficult."

He didn't seem to be able to talk to her without saying something that either was downright offensive or implied that she was doing something wrong. Maggie's temper rose.

"I'm not being difficult. This situation isn't my doing. The university made a mistake. I will handle it this week." She waved a hand around the shop. "First, I have to take care of my business, then I'll see to your professor's request. You say that only boxes with *SW* on them are the correct ones, but I don't know that for sure, and I would hate for another mistake to be made. I also don't feel comfortable with someone else handling my husband's things. I will go through everything I have from the university and make sure every box is accounted for."

Without a word, Conrad stepped away from the counter. A small pile of brochures on the area sat on its far edge. He picked up one on the birds of coastal Maine. He opened the pamphlet and studied the map inside.

"If you aren't going to let me do my job here, I might as well do some sightseeing," he said.

Relieved, Maggie picked up another brochure on the museums in the area. "You might be interested in this too." She proceeded to tell him about the most popular tourist sites in Somerset Harbor and adjacent towns.

He listened, took the pamphlet on museums, and added it to his bird brochure. He folded them and stuffed them into his back pocket. "I'll check back with you each day," he said. "Just in case your priorities change."

13

After a quiet Sunday spent at church and catching up on paperwork at home, Maggie was ready for her Monday outing to South Doe Island with Eric. The morning sun promised a warm day as Maggie drove to the dock, passing several houses with piles of lobster traps in their front and side yards. Pretty soon those traps would be spread throughout the waters, ensnaring the signature catch of the region.

She parked near a weathered clapboard building bearing a sign with the mail boat company's logo. Several people were already milling about, waiting to buy tickets for the morning boat. Eric leaned against the ticket booth's side wall, talking to a workman wearing overalls. As she approached, she saw a picture of a pipe and a sink on a red-and-orange box clutched in the workman's arm. *I'll bet he's a plumber going out to the island to make a service call.*

She joined Eric and a small cluster of passengers on the wharf and gazed out over the water toward the open sea.

"The captain said the island is almost thirty miles away," Eric said. "That's pretty far to come in case of an emergency."

Maggie looked at him and wondered if he was thinking of his father and his father's health.

"The peace and quiet that Mrs. Baranowski seeks comes at the price of convenience," she said. "But it's worth it to her."

"Would you want to live out there? Thirty miles away with no way back to the mainland except by boat?"

Maggie stared out over the wide expanse of water. "No,

I wouldn't. I would never want to be that far away from Emily. There would be no surprise visits, and emergencies could be a problem. Although in a crisis there's always a helicopter."

"Yeah, I guess." Eric pushed his hair back against the slight breeze that had come up.

"Still, even though I might not choose to live out there, I'm actually looking forward to our trip," she said. "We might find some lovely chests for the shop. And I hope we'll have some time to enjoy the wildlife on the island too."

Once Maggie had purchased the tickets, they had to wait for a while before the mail boat left. During that time, three men worked quickly and efficiently, moving back and forth between the boat and the parking area of the dock. They loaded wood boxes, bags of compost, manure, mulch, a bathroom sink, bananas, cases of dried milk, crackers, bread, vegetables, other grocery supplies, trays of small plants, and several pieces of luggage.

Maggie guessed that much of the cargo was to go to the island's small grocery store, or maybe its café, although she doubted whether the restaurant would be open yet, since it was too early in the season. Perhaps in another few weeks. Most small cafés closed for the winter months because there simply weren't enough customers to merit keeping them open. Daisy was lucky that The Busy Bean was popular enough for the locals to keep it open in the off-season.

Finally, an engine was lifted from the dock and onto the deck through a system of belts and pulleys. Eric watched the cargo being raised and lowered. "A truck engine," he said in amazement. "This mail boat really does deliver everything."

The line of passengers began to move down the ramp and step onto the boat. One couple had a basket, which Maggie guessed was for a picnic. Two bottles of sparkling water peeked out from under a cloth embroidered with lobsters. Several people appeared to be regulars. They talked freely to each other and to the three men packing the goods. A family with four children excitedly entered the protected area of the boat and settled down on its wooden bench along the side. In the middle, over the boat's engine, a platform held all of the boxes and bags Maggie had seen delivered earlier.

Maggie and Eric followed the family into the boat's interior. The room was surrounded by windows and housed the dashboard and ship wheel. Already in place were two of the men Maggie had watched loading the boat earlier. They turned out to be the captain and his mate. She could just barely see the third fellow outside still on the ramp, helping the last of the boarding passengers.

As she scanned the other boarders, she recognized a tall fellow in worn jeans and a plain blue shirt with its long sleeves rolled up to his elbows. Conrad.

Was he following her? No, that was silly. He probably just needed something to do and happened to pick this particular activity.

He never looked in the direction of the boat's cabin where she sat, for which she was foolishly glad. Once on board, he stepped up to the railing, leaned against it, and watched the captain's mate prepare the boat to leave the pier.

The roar of the boat's engine drew Maggie's attention to the front, where the captain had just started the motor. The other passengers responded by speaking more loudly to each other over the incessant, low rumble. Nevertheless, the engine's noise so dominated the cabin that their conversations were turned into muffled, meaningless sounds. At the same time, the engine also caused the boat to vibrate so much that Maggie's whole body shook in time with it.

As they began to glide out of the harbor, the captain's mate came around collecting tickets. Maggie gave him hers and Eric's, then settled in to try to enjoy the trip. She shifted slightly on the bench so that she could see out the windows behind her. Mesmerized by the seascape, she noted every tiny island they slid past, watched distant billowy clouds, and marveled at the barely distinct line separating the sea and sky.

Her clear sight of her surroundings didn't last long. They had hardly started into the ocean when fog seeped in around them, smudging her view of the buildings on shore. As the mist thickened, even the close islands on either side became barely discernible or were lost altogether. It was as if she were looking at these granite and tree-covered islands through smoked glass.

A few loons and a line of buoys soon became all Maggie could see. The overall effect was atmospheric and mystical, but she was glad to know the boat had a good GPS system. Virtually blind, the mail boat chugged through the dense fog at what Maggie thought was a rather fast speed.

"This boat can really move, but I hope the captain doesn't hit anything," Eric said, echoing her thoughts.

"They do this run twice a day, all year around. I'd like to think they know what they're doing."

Eric glanced at the captain at the wheel and the mate standing with a hip resting against a side cabinet. "Yeah, you're right. The good days are easy, but they can handle the tough days as well. Experience." He stared at the captain, who appeared to be in his early thirties. "I heard one of the other passengers say the captain has been doing this for years, but his mate is pretty new."

"Well, he has to learn somehow, and the boat is in the hands of the captain. I'm sure he could make this run in his sleep." Maggie smiled reassuringly.

"Right," Eric said, but his hand rubbing told Maggie he was still a bit nervous as they sped through the deep mist.

After sitting in the boat's cabin area for most of the trip,

Maggie was restless. Finally, the fog lessened and large patches of clear blue began to appear. Grabbing a nearby post, she rose and made her way to the open back of the boat on uncertain, wobbly legs. Eric followed her. As she made her unsteady way, she looped the strap of her small camera over her wrist. She wanted to take a few pictures to send Emily. Perhaps her daughter would like to take a trip out to the island when she came home for break this summer.

The couple she had seen with the picnic basket sat on the back bench. Both had large cameras with what Maggie could only describe as serious lenses clutched in their hands, at the ready for the perfect shot. A couple of men bent over the rails, looking out into the thick, cottony envelope. Conrad appeared to be engrossed in the fog-wrapped sea and the ghostly buoys and loons. He never looked in her direction.

Maggie leaned against the side to stabilize herself and turned toward the water, hoping to see a loon pop up again, or perhaps an island gently appearing from the mist. Eric joined her. As they looked out, the fog covered the boat.

"You may not have much luck taking any pictures," Eric said.

Holding her camera to her eye, Maggie pressed the shutter button. "The fog creates wonderful mood shots," she said. She pointed out into the water at a red-and-white-striped, bottle-shaped form bobbing in the water. "That buoy is more interesting now than if it were bright and sunny."

Eric shrugged. "I guess. I'd sure like to see where we're going, though. There could be an island right in front of us and we wouldn't know until we hit it."

She laughed. "That's why there are so many buoys to mark our path. And if we can't see those, every boat today has a GPS system."

He didn't look convinced and just glumly stared out into

the pale gray morass. After a few moments of silence, he moved around to the other side.

Soon Maggie became aware of a change in the engine noise level. They were slowing down. The sky once more opened up with bright blue patches breaking through the fog. South Doe Island appeared.

Standing on the side of the boat facing the shore, Maggie continued to take close-up pictures, mesmerized by the beauty of water breaking against the island's surrounding rocks and weather-worn pier. Several other passengers who had been sitting in the back seemed to be similarly enchanted by the view, and a small crowd gathered at the rail nearby.

Suddenly, the ship's deck jolted. As she was thrown toward the railing, her camera flew out of her hand. She madly fought rising panic as her chest lurched over the side of the boat and she came face-to-face with roiling, steel-gray water.

14

Clutching at the bar and catching her foot under the truck engine sitting in the middle, Maggie kept herself from falling out of the boat.

"Maggie!" Eric instantly appeared at her side and helped her back to the safe side of the railing. "I was just going inside when the boat hit something and I saw you start to fall."

Several other passengers, including the picnicking couple and the family of six, crowded around Maggie, some offering help and others asking if she was okay.

Shaking, Maggie shoved her hair back out of her eyes and grasped the camera dangling on her wrist from its looped cord. "I'm fine." Her breathing was fast, her heartbeat faster. "Thank you. What happened?"

Eric pointed to a pier running along the side of the boat. "The captain's mate was at the wheel and didn't calculate the boat's movement well enough to bring it in carefully. If you'd fallen, you could have been crushed between the boat and that pier."

Maggie stared at the thick, gray boards of the pier and their sturdy pillars. *Crushed.*

Looking up at Eric, she thought his eyes reflected concern. She relived the moment just before falling. The jolt was so sudden, so unexpected. She'd been looking through her viewfinder when the boat's port side abruptly hit the pier, knocking her off-balance.

She shut her eyes. She hadn't been the only one at the rail, so why had she been the only one who almost fell overboard? Other passengers had been near her. Had she felt a hand on her back? The boat had hit the wharf, but had someone helped her almost fall overboard? It had all happened in an instant and she couldn't remember the details exactly, except that she was focused on taking pictures of the approaching island and the docks.

She opened her eyes and surveyed the area around her. Eric was standing near her, but the other passengers had begun to line up to leave. Conrad stood second in line, just steps away from her, with a backpack hanging off one shoulder.

Where had he been when she almost fell? Maggie tried to remember, but she hadn't been paying attention. *Stop it, Maggie. He didn't try to push you overboard.* She tried to tell herself that it was a coincidence this ill-mannered man was on the same boat she'd nearly fallen from, but her suspicions had flared.

She calmed her breathing and shut off her camera, then looked at Eric. "Well, we're here and safe, in spite of the boat hitting the pier." She forced her voice to sound even.

The line of passengers began disembarking. Conrad glanced in her direction as he started filing past, but he didn't speak.

"Hi, Conrad," she said, trying to greet him with a light tone. She wasn't feeling particularly lighthearted at the moment, though. "What brings you here?"

Conrad's face was stony, but he answered her. "I heard you talk about South Doe Island when I was at the shop the other day. Apparently it's well known for its shorebirds, so I came to enjoy the sights. I'm what you'd call an avid birder." He patted his backpack. "Brought my camera to get some shots." He sounded like a typical tourist, not like a man with wicked intentions.

Well, why should he? Maggie chastised herself. Just because he seemed to dislike her, there was no reason to believe he had tried to push her overboard. She thrust the idea aside. Even though she considered it odd that he'd turn up on the same mail boat she and Eric were taking, that didn't mean Conrad was up to something nefarious.

"Well, I wish you well." Maggie forced a smile. "The weather certainly seems changeable, and the fog comes and goes quite often."

"Don't worry about that. The magic of mist. It might make the birds even more photogenic."

The exchange, brief though it was, caused the line to slow, and Maggie heard a few grumbles. He threw an apologetic look at those behind him. "Got to go." He stepped off the boat and climbed the steep incline to the street level.

Maggie watched him leave, then she and Eric gathered their few things together and joined the line.

Mrs. Baranowski waved to Maggie and Eric as they stepped off the boat and walked up the steps from the pier to where she stood.

"I live near here." She shot a glance at Maggie's feet and the black flats she wore with her neat jeans. She nodded approvingly. "I'm along the main street. It's an easy walk."

Maggie and Eric fell in with her as they strolled past several cottage-size houses. Mrs. Baranowski gave them a short history of the island and its recent development. She was as proud of the community as if she were a native and not a recent arrival.

They ambled down a street that hugged the coastline. The side of the road along the water held a smattering of houses placed on parcels of land barely large enough to build on. A continuous, rather haphazard row of modest houses lined the other side. A small white church with a square bell tower loomed ahead on a road bearing to the left up a steep hill.

"That's Chapel Street. My home is on the other side of the church."

As they rounded the corner, Mrs. Baranowski's cottage came into view. It lacked the gingerbread details of the Somerset

Harbor houses, but the compact, beige clapboard building with white trim and a small porch was tidy, sturdy, and welcoming.

Mrs. Baranowski led them through the front door into a surprisingly airy room with a bank of windows looking out over the ocean. Bookshelves ran along the wall under them. The windowless wall opposite brimmed with abstract paintings and groupings of framed family photos. The walls were painted the most intense glossy white Maggie had ever seen used in a house. She thought it made both a perfect backdrop to the pictures and an ideal frame for nature's greens and blues outside the window. Rugs were scattered over a broad-planked wood floor. A love seat and two upholstered chairs surrounded one rug near the bank of windows, providing the occupants a view of greenery and water. A round dining table sat to one side.

"This is my everything room," Mrs. Baranowski said cheerfully. "And this"—she passed through another door—"is my kitchen and sleeping area."

Maggie stepped into the next space while Eric remained in the doorway. It would have been a bit tight with all three of them in the room together. In this area, the walls were a warm rust color, and the woodwork and ceiling were all the same incredible glossy white as the other room. A door leading out to an inviting patio separated a kitchen area from an iron-framed daybed set against the wall.

"Did you say kitchen *and* sleeping area?" Maggie raised her eyes at the daybed, which was covered in bright pillows, then gave Mrs. Baranowski a quizzical look.

The older woman grinned. "I told you my place was cozy. I actually like this arrangement. I can recline while reading, enjoy the view, and keep an eye on my food cooking on the stove at the same time." The bell-like sound of her laughter filled the room.

"I'm glad it works so well for you," Maggie said.

"Have a seat." Mrs. Baranowski waved toward the small table in the other room. "I'll get us some tea. After that boat ride, you're both probably a little chilled."

Maggie was chilled, and not only from the cold.

Before leaving the kitchen to join Eric at the small dining table, Maggie turned to the sprightly woman. "Can I do anything?"

"No thanks. You two sit. After you have tea and warm up, I'll take you out to the garage to see the chests."

A little while later, the trio trekked outside. Mrs. Baranowski hadn't brought a car to the island, so the garage had become her storage area. And it was packed. When she pushed the door up, a solid wall of boxes and antique furniture prevented them from entering. Fortunately, the chests were stacked up on one side. Braided rugs separated one chest from another, preventing scratches, just as Maggie had seen in the pictures Mrs. Baranowski had shown her in the shop.

Eric whistled. "Whoa, you've got the mother lode in here."

Maggie shot him a reprimanding look. He looked away, but she saw the amusement in his eyes. Giving the overstuffed garage another glance, she turned aside herself, hiding a grin. Eric was right. This was overwhelming. No wonder Mrs. Baranowski was willing to sell her chests.

Working together, Eric and Maggie disentangled three of the trunks from the surrounding items. After some shuffling, a New England blanket chest, a Korean chest with brass details, and an old painted pine chest rested in a neat row in front of them. After carefully examining them for authenticity and good condition, Maggie purchased all three.

Mrs. Baranowski, who had anticipated that Maggie would want them, called her neighbor. A grizzled fellow in his late fifties showed up with an old Ford pickup truck, and he and Eric loaded the chests in the truck's bed for transporting to the dock.

The truck only had room for two in the cab, so Eric went in the pickup and the two women walked to the pier along a picturesque route that followed the ocean.

When they stopped to admire the view, Maggie was enchanted. Not being up on her shorebirds, she couldn't identify the species flying and walking about the sand, but she still enjoyed watching them, with their quick, spindly legs and plump bodies. Some appeared to run randomly about the shore as if excited just to be there. Others swooped into the sparkling waters, probably hunting for dinner.

A lone figure of a man, pressed up against a large rock and holding a black camera to his face, was the only nonbird on the shoreline. His whole body showed intense involvement.

Maggie could easily tell that it was Conrad. Perhaps he really had come to photograph the wildlife and not to follow her. She sighed. When was she being overly suspicious and when should she be more observant and careful? It was a difficult balance. She wanted to trust in people, to believe in their goodness. At the same time, as recent events proved, she couldn't stick her head in the sand either.

Mrs. Baranowski seemed to notice her transformed mood. "Is there something the matter, dear?"

Maggie smiled wanly. "No, not really." Changing the subject, she said, "I can see why you enjoy living here. It really is beautiful and peaceful."

The retired schoolteacher took a deep breath, inhaling the salted air. "I do love this little island, but small beauties are everywhere. Your Somerset Harbor is a treasure too."

Maggie grinned at her again, this time with true contentment. "It certainly is."

The two women stood in companionable silence, looking out over the shoreline. Maggie watched Conrad. He seemed to be in a state of intense repose. An oxymoron, she mused, much like the way she was beginning to see him.

After a while, the ladies slowly began their stroll back down the narrow road to the dock, where Eric was waiting next to the chests.

As Maggie had expected, Conrad was among the passengers on the afternoon boat. If he had missed the return trip, he would have had to stay overnight on the island and wait for the next day's mail boat. From what Maggie could see, there were no hotels, and she didn't notice any bed-and-breakfast signs posted in front of anyone's home. Those passengers staying overnight or for a few days must have made prior arrangements with a townsperson.

This time, when he saw her, he came over to where she stood with Eric, waiting to board. "Good area for catching sight of the shorebirds," he said, holding what looked to Maggie to be a professional camera.

Eric noticed his equipment too. "That's quite a camera. I'm more a point-and-shoot kind of guy. In fact, my phone is usually my camera." He tapped his front pocket where he kept his cell phone.

"I use this to document site information when we're digging," Conrad said. "And I also have a longtime interest in birds. I have had several of my photographs published in nature magazines." A distinctive note of pride colored his words.

Maggie studied him as if seeing a new person behind the irritating, irascible man he normally appeared to be—a young man who was excited about fully experiencing the world around him.

As if he'd exposed too much, Conrad stiffened. "Guess we can board," he said, then gave them a curt nod and stomped away toward the mail boat.

Maggie and Eric remained on the dock, watching the captain and his mate finish loading Mrs. Baranowski's chests.

Once all three chests were sitting side by side on deck, the captain said to Maggie, "All set. No rain on the way back, only fog, so there's no need to cover them."

She nodded and sat on a bench, facing the trunks.

"Nice haul," Conrad said, eyeing Maggie's purchases. He stood at the railing nearby.

I guess he's decided he can talk to us again. This man certainly runs hot and cold.

"Where are you going to put them? You seem to like fancy displays. How many of these can you put in one?"

"We'll store them and display one at a time," Maggie said.

"Of course," he said. "You have that storage area upstairs."

A loon gave a call from the water. Conrad turned out toward the ocean, sighted the loon with his camera, and began clicking away.

Maggie squinted at Conrad's profile, dark against the sunlight reflecting off the water. *Why would he mention that? Has he been up there?*

As if forgetting Maggie and Eric were there, Conrad moved to the rearmost point of the boat and sat down, body turned toward the churning sea at the boat's stern, camera ready.

Eric walked into the boat's interior. Maggie leaned back and put her shoes up on the raised platform in the center. She let the sun fall full onto her face, closed her eyes, and felt the boat undulating under her. The constant noise of its engine contrasted with the lighter sounds of the churning waves.

Shortly, Eric rejoined Maggie on the bench.

"There's a better view from here," he said, facing out. The sunlight glanced off the gray-blue water, highlighting the tops of its ripples. A pair of loons bobbed silently alongside.

Maggie adjusted herself so that she could also look out to the ever-changing sea. And this time, she made sure to anchor herself firmly in case of any more unexpected jolts by the boat—or anyone attempting to push her overboard.

15

Tuesday passed as any other day, but to Maggie it seemed unbearably slow. Later, after the shop closed, she planned to attack those confounded boxes of Richard's.

After locking up for the night, Maggie made her way up the stairs to the carriage house attic. She felt uncommonly tired. Perhaps, she reasoned, it was because this task weighed heavily on her heart. To be honest, as she reflected on the perfectly normal day she'd had, there was no other objective reason for her exhaustion.

She stopped at the attic entrance and, leaning against the doorway, surveyed the room crowded with containers of all shapes and sizes, including the crates and boxes holding her husband's work. She entered and pulled every one of Richard's boxes into the room's center. Most of the wooden boxes weighed more than she could easily lift. Other boxes were simply too unwieldy given their combination of size and weight. So she shoved them all, scraping over the floor, into the center.

Using a crowbar, she opened each of the wooden crates. Many were filled with shredded newspaper and held marked brown paper bags filled with broken chunks of brick, glass, and porcelain. The notations gave the fragments' precise location and date when found, along with initials for the site.

Other wooden boxes held an array of hand tools as well as a couple of fold-up rulers for measuring the height of a pit or the dimensions of a stain in the ground. Each implement was now clean and shiny with no dried dirt clinging to its worn blade.

Amid the tools and paper-bagged specimens, Maggie also discovered some of Richard's handwritten notes. As she ran a finger over his penmanship, she remembered Richard's enthusiasm for the historical sites he'd worked on in Virginia and Pennsylvania. He always stressed the importance of keeping accurate notes and documentation. "Good record keeping," he liked to say, "is the backbone for all fieldwork and imperative to every successful project."

A stain was often all his team would find—a discoloration of the soil left to posterity from what was once an ancient trash pit or a post hole or an old wooden wall. Those stains were as important to Richard as the beautiful Anasazi pottery apparently was to Professor Faber. They told a story about a people no longer able to speak for themselves. These marks reached out to others across time and proved those people had not disappeared into nothingness, that they had lived, and loved, and died.

That had been Richard's life—connecting to the past. The human past. It was what he always wanted to, and did, share with her.

After finishing with the wooden crates, Maggie reopened the first cardboard box she had delved into last week, which had been originally addressed to Richard at the university and then sent to their home address. She reached into the envelope marked *Confidential* and pulled out the ledger-style notes. As she did, a smaller white paper fell out of the envelope. She caught it before it had fluttered all the way to the floor. She examined it, eyes widening as she read Richard's handwritten note:

If anything untoward or suspicious happens to me, protect my family from harm.

RW

Maggie's heart pounded and her head spun. The words *protect my family* reeled through her mind. Richard had died a natural death from an aortic aneurysm—there was no doubt about that. And yet, this note indicated that he had been involved in something quite dangerous.

Maggie crumpled to the floor. The paper trembled in her hands. The room seemed to pulsate around her as she came to grips with this latest discovery.

Finally, she roused herself. She reread the note and then pulled back the box's flaps. Inside, a black-on-white rim peeked up through the packing peanuts.

Maggie stood up and once more scrutinized the boxes she had pulled out. She began to systematically separate out the cardboard containers. Those without the *SW* marking went on the opposite wall, and those with *SW* remained in the center. In the end, she had a line of fifteen slightly battered, heavy-duty corrugated cardboard boxes of various sizes clustered together, all with *SW* on their sides.

As she surveyed her work, her stomach growled. She checked her watch and saw that it was past eight. She wanted to delve into the boxes more, to open each one up, looking for Richard's notes and examining the other contents. By now, though, she truly was drained of energy, and any ability to focus had waned. Scary as the note was, Maggie told herself, these boxes with their secrets had been sitting here for years. They could wait a bit longer.

Maggie trudged back to the manor. Snickers sat just within the doorway, waiting for attention. She ruffled his fur quickly and made for the kitchen, where she reheated some soup for dinner.

As she finished her soup, the phone rang. Maggie immediately recognized Ina's strong voice.

"Any word on the intrusion the other night?" Ina cut right to the chase. "Nothing reported on the scanner."

Maggie sighed. "Officer Clayton phoned earlier and updated me on the police findings. Which she said remains at nothing."

"Well, I'm always ready to help if you need me," Ina said. "Just call. And keep that flashlight close."

Maggie reassured her that everything was fine and that she'd certainly contact her if needed. Then she had a thought. Maybe her friends could help her decode Richard's notes.

"Say, Ina, do you think you could help me figure something out?"

"Maggie, that is a silly question. I'm always up for some detective work. What's the case?"

Maggie smiled. "You're right—I should always assume you're up for a challenge. Instead of telling you about it now, can you meet me at the historical society tomorrow morning? I'm going to see if I can get the other ladies to help too."

"It must be a real doozy if you need all of us. I'll be there."

"Thanks, Ina. You're a lifesaver."

Maggie hung up, then phoned her other friends in the historical society and repeated what she'd asked Ina, telling them that she thought they would be able to use their research skills to solve a mystery.

Everyone planned to come except Daisy and June. Daisy couldn't leave the café during that busy time of the day, so Maggie promised to come to The Busy Bean after the meeting and update her. She told June, who was expecting a delivery at the shop, the same thing.

With her friends signed on to help, Maggie felt more optimistic about solving this mystery. She only hoped it didn't prove that her husband had been up to something nefarious before his death.

After washing out her soup bowl, Maggie went to her office, sat down at her desk, and turned on the computer. As she waited for it to boot up, she watched Snickers settle down next to her. He climbed into the small cat bed Maggie kept nearby, circled a couple of times, and curled up. Maggie only wished she could do the same. Go to bed and sleep. But checking her e-mail one last time in the evening had become a habit and she didn't break it tonight.

Opening her e-mail account, the first thing that caught Maggie's eye was another message from the university departmental secretary. She groaned. The bright screen stared silently back at her. She clicked on the e-mail and it opened.

. The secretary apologized again for the error the archaeology lab had made by sending the wrong materials to Maggie. She reiterated that Professor Faber—with whom Richard had been collaborating on a professional book—knew precisely which items were mistakenly sent. Although the publication had been on hold, Professor Faber had been approached to present an analysis and his findings at an upcoming international symposium, and he now needed the materials back with all haste.

In order to simplify things for Maggie, the secretary went on, Professor Faber had arranged for his assistant to go to Somerset Harbor. He might have contacted her by now. If he hadn't, he would shortly.

Maggie sat back and glared at the screen. *Conrad has been in town since Thursday.* Didn't the office know that? He'd arrived much too early to collect the materials. Now Maggie wondered if the professor knew that his assistant was already in town.

She worried her lower lip, lost in thought. Maybe there'd been a communication problem and Conrad had misunderstood the time frame.

She felt the irritation that had been developing toward the university and Faber float away. Conrad had jumped the gun. Leaning forward again, she continued reading the e-mail.

When Conrad Boynton arrives, Professor Faber would appreciate it if you have the Southwestern artifacts and materials ready for him to pick up and bring back to the university's archaeology lab.

Thank you for seeing to this problem as soon as possible.

Regards,

Betsy Hanover, secretary

Department of Archaeology and Anthropology

The note was quite civil. Still, there seemed to have been a mix-up in the timetable, in what Maggie thought she'd told Faber. But she was glad to know he had not completely ignored the fact that she had needed time. Apparently, both the university and Faber thought Conrad had just arrived or would arrive soon. In her opinion, their lines of communication seemed tenuous at best.

Maggie looked at the calendar on her computer. It was already Tuesday evening. She couldn't possibly have everything ready for him any earlier than this weekend. Even the weekend felt too soon, she admitted to herself. Her sense of loss over Richard's death had been renewed this week, and she wasn't sure she was ready to let go of anything related to him. Those plain cardboard boxes were more than just containers for antiquities—they tied her to her past.

She quickly wrote a reply. She politely conveyed that, due to previous commitments, she had not been able to get to Richard's boxes before now. She assured the secretary that she would definitely go through them in earnest soon. She understood the professor needing the antiquities back, but his assistant had been sent prematurely. She'd let him know as soon as possible when the materials could be picked up.

She hit *Send*, rested her elbow on the desk, and placed her hand over her eyes.

. . . .

Sleep wouldn't come. No matter how weary she was, Maggie couldn't shake the unsettled feeling that had crept back under her skin after receiving the secretary's e-mail. Her need to find out why her husband had felt compelled to write that warning note was growing by the minute.

After exchanging her pajamas for jeans and a sweatshirt, Maggie returned to the antiques shop attic intent on going through the rest of Richard's things. More heavy-duty cardboard boxes with *SW* in black marker sat in the center of the floor, securely taped shut, challenging her to look inside them.

When she opened the closest box and thrust aside the protective foam, she found two more Anasazi pots. Another envelope marked *Confidential* in Richard's handwriting had been tucked inside. She stared at it. Was it another warning, a message about possible danger?

With her heart pounding and head buzzing, Maggie removed the note and read: *SWC—MD. One Sosi black-on-white bowl, nine inches in diameter, ca. AD 1070–1180. One Sosi black-on-white pitcher, seven and a half inches high, ca. AD 1070–1180*, plus a dollar amount for each. She placed the note back on top of the packing material and went on to open another.

In each box with *SW* written on its side she found more pottery and other early Southwestern artifacts as well as the now-expected envelope marked *Confidential*. In the largest box, along with pieces of pottery, she found a list with dates, telephone numbers, and e-mail addresses. Several items had a checkmark next to them. In reviewing the list, she realized that the checked items were the artifacts she'd seen in the boxes.

Maggie sat in the harsh glare of the overhead light and wondered why Richard had such a list. What did all the notes mean? The descriptions and prices were obvious, but what about the initials? She placed the list on the top of a box and surveyed the opened containers surrounding her, as if an answer would come to her if she stared hard enough.

She pressed her lips together, thinking. When they were younger, she had joined Richard in some archaeological work in Peru and Central America, but that had been a long time ago, early in his career, when they were first married. Eventually, he had settled on specializing in the historical archaeology of the Eastern United States. He had never worked on or shown much interest in researching Southwest archaeology.

It was confusing. Professor Faber said they had been doing a book together, something she'd never heard about. Why would Richard coauthor something outside his area of expertise? Certainly he had had plenty of work to do in his chosen field, where he was highly regarded. And why wouldn't he tell her about it?

Maggie gazed at the line of boxes she'd assembled. She couldn't deny the existence of this Southwestern pottery and its connection with her husband. The mailing labels under the university's label proved they had all been sent specifically to him. The notes testified to his having done at least some initial analysis. Why hadn't he ever mentioned this to her?

And then there was the warning Richard had written about his family's safety.

A knot grew in Maggie's chest. What had he been involved with? Had their relationship so deteriorated that he had no longer felt he could share his passions with her? The thought was like a rubber band constricting around her heart.

She looked at the unwelcome interlopers masked as innocent prehistoric pottery. Where did Professor Faber come into the picture? So far, she hadn't found anything even mentioning his name or referring to him. Yet the university said these items belonged to him.

Clearly, she wasn't going to find any answers tonight. Perhaps her morning meeting with her friends would yield better results, especially now that Maggie had gathered several more pages of Richard's notes. She closed and locked the attic door behind her and returned the key to a hook in the workroom. She checked every window and door to the shop to make sure they were secured, then turned off the lights and walked out the door, locking it firmly behind her. Mind swimming, she trudged home in the dark, still night.

16

Arriving at the historical society building the next morning, Maggie found Ruth in the dining room setting out a carafe of coffee and several mugs for the meeting. Maggie had no sooner poured herself a cup than Ina, Fran, and Liz bustled in, chattering excitedly.

After everyone settled in, Maggie explained about the university's e-mails, about the many Southwestern artifacts worth thousands of dollars among her husband's belongings, and the insistent Professor Faber. To wrap up, she said, "I told the professor that his assistant could pick up the antiquities this weekend. I'm working on going through all the boxes that seem to have Southwestern artifacts packed in them. But I don't really want to let them go before I find out why Richard was involved with all of this and maybe even why he didn't tell me."

The ladies, all listening intently, nodded.

Maggie tucked her hair behind her ear. "Here's where you come in. What I would like is for you all to use your research skills to help me decode Richard's notes. There's something about this whole thing that bothers me. I admit that I'm confused. I don't really know what I'm looking for or what it will mean. Somehow, however, I do believe his notes hold the key to the Anasazi pottery mystery." She looked around the table, making eye contact with each woman. "Will you help me?"

"Of course!"

"This will be fun!"

"We've needed a new project!"

"Thought you'd never ask!"

Everyone in the group responded enthusiastically, embracing the challenge.

Maggie smiled at their unreserved willingness to ferret out the meaning behind Richard's notes. What she didn't tell them was that she had a growing sense of unease that she might not like what they found out. With a quick twitch of her head, she flipped that disloyal thought away.

"I made several photocopies of the list for you to work with," she said, reaching into a file folder and handing out a sheet to each woman.

After reviewing the list and asking questions about what Maggie already knew, which wasn't much, they dug into the project. Maggie thanked her friends and left them to it.

. . . .

As Maggie walked the few blocks to The Busy Bean to talk with Daisy, she let her mind go over the unpleasant events of the past week or two. First there had been the near miss with the car outside the museum, then the break-ins at the manor and the shop. There had been the frightening incident on the boat in which she'd almost fallen—or been pushed—overboard. And then there was the note from Richard about his family's safety.

What are the common denominators? Eric and Conrad had both been on the boat, and both men had been milling around her property the night of the tour, before the shop had been invaded. But the day the manor had been broken into, Conrad hadn't even been in town yet, to Maggie's knowledge, and Eric had only just learned about the Southwestern pottery in her attic the day before.

Both men, different as could be in their personalities, had a strong interest in the boxes and their contents. Conrad's seemed fully professional, but his hostility toward Maggie made her question the lengths he might go to in order to get his professor's property back.

Eric, on the other hand, was overly enthusiastic—but what motivated him? Was it the historical value of these antiquities that enchanted him, or was it their monetary worth? And she couldn't forget about the mystery class he claimed to be taking or his absences from work. Or the fact that she'd seen him with the young reporter, Connie, when he claimed he'd forgotten he had a shift scheduled and was studying.

Trying to dispel the unease that had plagued her for days, Maggie held her head high as she entered The Busy Bean. As she expected, the café was quiet at this hour. There were only four tables with customers: two couples and two solo customers—a single woman and a single man—all looking like tourists visiting Somerset Harbor.

She glanced at the man again. She'd seen him in her shop and around town over the last few days. He didn't notice her as he devoured a piece of Boston cream pie. Maggie blanched slightly at this surprising choice for so early in the morning.

Jenny easily cared for all of the customers with brisk efficiency, allowing Maggie to tell Daisy everything about finding the pots and her husband's notes. After answering Daisy's thoughtful questions, she gave her a copy of Richard's list and left for the antiques shop.

When Maggie entered the shop a few minutes later, there were several customers milling about. She spied Connie, camera hanging off her shoulder and notebook in hand. The reporter seemed to be looking in Maggie's direction, so Maggie waved a hello. Connie turned slightly without responding, aiming her camera at an Early American pewter dinner set.

Surprised by Connie apparently ignoring her greeting, Maggie wondered whether she had imagined it or if the young woman was avoiding her. *Perhaps she's just focused on getting more pictures for her article.* She wondered how much was enough for the article anyway. She should have had plenty of material for the newspaper. The History by Candlelight Tour had been several days ago, so it was practically old news by now.

Maggie was about to approach Connie when she noticed Eric talking with another browser nearby. The man wore a tan jacket over a blue shirt. A worn, brimmed hat dangled from his right hand. Trying not to stare, Maggie surreptitiously examined him. *Isn't he the man who was at The Busy Bean just a little while ago?*

She pursed her lips in thought. A lot of tourists were in town, but she was sure she'd seen him at least a couple of times in her shop and on Friday evening too. The mint man.

As far as she could remember, he hadn't bought anything. Yet he kept coming back. Maybe he had his eye on an expensive antique in the shop but wasn't yet ready to pull the trigger, so to speak.

Maggie walked in their direction, hoping to get close enough to listen in on their conversation and, if possible, politely inquire whether she could help the mint man with something in particular. With all the strange things happening lately, she wanted to know more about this guy who kept popping up.

As Maggie approached, she caught some of their conversation. "My wife loves antiques shops," the mint man said. "She usually browses and—I hate to admit it—impulse buys." He snickered. "I'm more focused. I'm really only interested in Native American artifacts."

"Native American stuff is harder to find in our area," Eric said. "I understand antiques shops in the Midwest and West often have a lot more. The East has been settled for so long, most of what you'll find is European or Early American stuff."

Eric sure has learned a lot about the business in just a little while, Maggie mused with a sense of pride.

The customer made a sorrowful face. "Yes, but I'm afraid I don't travel much. By scouring antiques shops, I've been able to find a few pieces for my collection. I'm always on the lookout."

Maggie paused, straightening out a few items on top of a dresser, all the while straining to catch every word.

The fellow went on. "I don't see any Native American artifacts or pottery here. Do you know of any place in the area that sells them?"

Eric perked up. "The owner of this shop has a bunch of prehistoric First American artifacts, including pots from the Southwest." Then he frowned. "But I don't know if she'd sell them."

"Ah, I am particularly interested in Southwestern pottery, especially early Pueblo pots. They're not easy to find anymore, and almost impossible to get out here. Do you know their provenance? Often sellers pass off reproductions as the real thing."

"You don't have to worry about that," Eric said, his voice eager and excited. "Her husband was an archaeologist. I'm sure she's got the real deal. I can find out more for you, if you want."

Their voices dropped so that Maggie could not hear more. Her hand involuntarily gripped a perfume decanter she had started to move on the display. Her eyes narrowed as she stared into the mirror, watching Eric and his companion as they talked. She began to regret letting him peek at the pots when he'd helped her move those boxes.

And what right did he have to say anything about them one way or the other? Then she recalled how wistful Eric sounded the other day when he talked about his own desire to possess such treasures. Selling them could solve a lot of his money concerns.

Finally, the stranger wandered down the aisle and Eric went back to cleaning a glass case. Maggie strode up to him.

Before she could say anything about his conversation with the customer, however, Eric opened with "I'm so glad to see you."

"Oh?"

"June had me doing some work over by the newest displays, and I've noticed several people hanging around them and acting strange."

"Strange?" Maggie nearly rolled her eyes, thinking that the words *suspicious* and *strange* were taking over her life. "What do you mean?"

"There are a lot of tempting small things in those displays, and some people spend a lot of time there, handling pocketable stuff. It would be easy to shoplift something. The adult master bedroom has lots of silver antiques on the vanity, the dining room has silver and porcelain pieces, and the child's bedroom has a bunch of smaller things too—maybe not valuable, but flashy."

Relieved at his answer, Maggie shook her head. "Touching things is natural. If you're worried about a particular person, just watch them. Do it carefully though, because you very well may be wrong about their intentions. We don't want shoplifters, that's for sure, but keep in mind what my Aunt Evelyn always said: The purpose of the vignettes is to entice and enchant."

"I know, but look at this." Eric led her to the child's bedroom. When they arrived, he pointed to the jewels hanging out of the chest. "This looks different. I think something is missing, but I can't remember exactly how it looked before."

Maggie studied the scene. The jewels cascading out of the pirate chest had been tampered with, she could tell. The pearl necklace with the large, gem-encrusted pendant was missing.

She looked closer. A long, multistring pearl necklace streamed out of the chest and onto the floor. That was new. She hadn't put it there. The bejeweled tiara and several brooches were still scattered at the base of the chest.

Maggie glanced at Eric, perplexed. There had been so many strange happenings, but this really made no sense. "You're right. A faux pearl necklace with a pendant is missing. And that long strand of pearls is new." She frowned. "Who would take one worthless necklace and replace it with another?"

Eric shrugged. "A child?"

"No, I don't think so. This is an exchange. It took forethought." Maggie shook her head. "This was a good catch, Eric. Keep an eye open for other incidents of theft and let June or me know immediately. It's a good thing you noticed the necklace was missing. Thanks for being so observant." Looking away, then back at Eric, she added, "I would like to speak with you later before you leave for the day." She hated having to reprimand him, but she didn't want him talking about Richard's things and giving false hope to customers. If she parted with that pottery, it would be to send it back to the university, where it apparently belonged.

"Sure, boss."

As he turned back to his work, Maggie caught a glimpse of Connie at the nearby setup of a home library. Camera in one hand, she adjusted the large equipment bag threatening to slip off her shoulder. She appeared to be completely consumed by the Edwardian mahogany desk set and kept fiddling with the camera's lens as if perfecting an image. Maggie walked over and greeted her. Connie barely lifted her head from her viewfinder as she gave a quick wave in return. Her intensity had formed a barrier against any intrusions.

Finally, after snapping one last shot, she let the camera hang off her shoulder and turned to Maggie with a tense smile on her face.

"You're really doing a lot of work for the newspaper," Maggie said. "I can't wait to see the article."

"I'm planning on doing a short series if my editor lets me." Connie had hardly gotten the sentence out when her cell phone rang. After a quick look at the phone's screen, she said, "I have to get this. Sorry."

Maggie nodded and ambled on, moving down the aisles. As she approached the front, her own cell phone rang. *These things are like having another person constantly following you around*, she thought as she answered it.

"We have some very interesting news about your codes," Ruth said. She couldn't hide the excitement in her voice.

"What did you find?" Maggie's heart jumped. Had her friends already come through?

"I believe we figured out what the initials mean. Can you come right over to the society building?"

Maggie quickly agreed and dashed out the door.

Four sets of eyes, all sparkling with excitement, greeted her as she stepped into the historical society library. Immediately, Ruth, Ina, Fran, and Liz began talking at once, their voices falling over each other in their excitement about their findings.

"We were able to get in touch with museum curators."

"The staff knew so much."

"They keep a record of all researchers who come to their museum."

"Dr. Linen was so . . ."

"Once the receptionist . . ."

Their united message was clear, even though their cacophony of voices was not: They had broken Richard's code.

Pleased to hear they'd been successful, Maggie took a seat at the table. Ruth clapped her hands and requested quiet from the group. A restrained silence prevailed. Their delight couldn't be so easily tempered, however, which was obvious as they each sat forward in their chairs, arms resting on the table, practically bursting with more to say. Ruth spoke for them.

As if giving a demonstration, Ruth took a note from the pile of paper in front of her and held it up. Maggie recognized it immediately. It read:

SWC—MD. One Sosi black-on-white bowl, nine inches in diameter, ca. AD 1070–1180. One Sosi black-on-white pitcher, seven and a half inches high, ca. AD 1070–1180.

"We've discovered that the first set of initials indicate college names," Ruth said.

"That's terrific," Maggie said, even though that didn't tell her much.

Ruth went on. "What's even more important is that each college mentioned has a small museum of local history and prehistory."

Now Maggie perked up.

"But there's more," Ina said.

Ruth tucked her hair behind her ears. "What Ina means is that we think we've also discovered that the rest of the initials belong to known First American collectors and their locations. This one, for instance, means Smith-Warren College and Marshall DeWitt." She paused. "So far that's all we have, but we were sure you'd want to know."

Impressed at their quick and efficient work, Maggie agreed. Progress was progress.

· · · · · · · · · · · · · · · · ·

Later that evening, Maggie sat in her kitchen sipping tea and mulling over the day. As she replayed her visit with the historical society crew, her eyes glowed. Her friends might very well have found the who of Richard's mystery. *But what about the why and how?*

She glanced down at the cup nesting in her hands. The mug was the one her husband had given her. Its worn logo peeked through her fingers. Richard's university's logo. The image made her pause.

As quickly as the excitement of fully realizing that her friends could trace the pottery and its provenance sank in, worry also filled her. Had Richard received these antiquities illegally? And had he been involved in selling them?

She stared unseeing at the dull green logo locked within her fingers. Where was her curiosity leading her?

17

"Hi, Maggie," Ina said cheerfully as Maggie opened her front door. The early morning sun highlighted the older woman's downy white hair as she bobbed her head in greeting. "I was out for a constitutional and thought I'd pop in to see how you were doing."

Maggie gladly welcomed her into the manor. *Ina is becoming quite the guardian angel.*

As they sat in the sunny kitchen enjoying coffee and slices of Maggie's homemade bread with blueberry jam, Ina chatted cheerfully about her favorite topic—Somerset Harbor's families and history. Maggie loved to learn about the community she'd adopted, and nobody told better stories about it than this bantam-like woman.

"Now, Eric's family is one of those early ones," Ina said. She took an appreciative bite of her bread, chewed it thoughtfully, and followed up with a sip of coffee. "I suppose you know about his family situation. About his father being chronically ill. Poor man can't work much due to his health and is seriously in debt. I know him. His predicament hurts his pride. The Clarks have always been a proud family." She wagged her bread. "Hardworking and proud."

"Eric told me he's been living at home since he left the military," Maggie said.

"His moving home has been a godsend to Mr. Clark. Of course, nothing around here pays much, and Eric is always looking for extra work, trying to find ways to make ends meet." Ina swung her bread around again. "And he's ambitious. You probably know he's back in school. Young people need a degree nowadays if they're going to get a decent job."

Maggie started to feel uncomfortable with Ina's talk about Eric, so she simply nodded without saying anything. Ina loved her town and its people. Maggie wasn't going to throw a wrench into things for her by talking about Eric's bogus class or her own growing discomfort over his interest in her husband's Native American artifacts.

Fortunately, speaking of Eric seemed to remind Ina of the antiques shop, and she changed topics. "That pirate motif you have for the child's room simply captivates me. I want to get a porthole mirror for a friend of mine. She has a granddaughter who'd love it. The child reads adventure stories all the time. She's even written about a cat that travels to Fiji by accidentally falling asleep in a suitcase." She chuckled. "It's all of three pages long. The longest story she's written so far. Granted, she's just seven years old."

After their coffee, the two strolled over to Carriage House Antiques in companionable silence. As they walked along, Maggie mulled over Ina's new information about Eric's need for money to cover his father's debts. *His money problems must be even bigger than I'd imagined.*

Would Eric consider stealing the pottery to solve his financial concerns? With his outgoing personality and tendency to make friends easily, it was possible he knew people who would be willing to pay him a lot of money for the artifacts in Richard's boxes, no questions asked.

Although she didn't want to suspect Eric of the break-ins, the chance that he'd been involved kept creeping back into her mind. She couldn't ignore the possibility.

On the other hand, she reminded herself, except for a few late days, he had been a hard worker and never complained. It wasn't fair to find him guilty based only on flimsy circumstantial evidence.

As seemed to be happening to her so often lately, questions without answers simply turned into more questions.

Ina and Maggie hadn't been in the shop long when Connie entered, toting her ubiquitous camera and camera bag, notebook in hand. The journalist came straight over to them, surprising Maggie.

Ever the curious historian, Ina lost little time before she began quizzing the young woman about her parents' families. An exhaustive and convoluted discussion of kinship relationships followed, involving who had married whom and who was the child of which parents. The two discovered that Ina had known Connie's grandparents years before. Connie's mom had moved to a nearby mill town when she married, and that was where Connie had grown up and gone to school. Her mother's family had been among the original settlers who founded Somerset Harbor.

At first, Connie appeared taken aback by Ina's recounting of past friendships and various kin ties on Connie's side. Eventually, however, she warmed up to the conversation and earnestly joined in. Maggie, lost in the minutia of their recollections, freed herself and went to help June.

Soon after, Ina left and Connie again wandered around the shop, taking close-up photos. As the young woman bent toward a crystal set, Maggie again wondered what was taking her so long in gathering material for her newspaper article. At this rate, Maggie calculated, she would only make a few cents per photo.

Connie stopped by to talk to her once more before leaving. Maggie asked how things were going and if there was anything more she could do for her.

"No thank you. I'm really just wrapping up. My editor did say he might be interested in a couple of articles for the newspaper." Connie's face lit up. "They always need filler, and this might be perfect." With that, she waved and left.

Maggie watched her go. The scrape of a wooden ladder being dragged into the workroom made her turn around. Eric had replaced an overhead light bulb and was putting the ladder away. Seeing him made her think about Connie's visit today. While in the shop, the girl had kept her distance from Eric, not even speaking to him. Quite different from her former visits, when they definitely seemed to be on friendly terms.

She still had to speak to him about his talking so freely about her personal things and the Indian antiquities. Should she do it now? She dreaded the thought.

An elderly man approached, asking if the shop had any old-style canes. With this welcome interruption, Maggie decided to talk to Eric later.

. . . .

In the middle of the afternoon, Maggie received a call from Professor Faber. As soon as he had identified himself, she launched into an update, her tone more defensive than she intended it to be. "I've been opening Richard's boxes, targeting those with SW marked on their sides," she said. "They seemed to be the only ones out of place with Richard's own former work."

"Isn't that what Conrad told you?" Professor Faber said. "He can take over now since you recognize that those are our boxes. We'll just have time to complete our study. The upcoming symposium is approaching quickly." His tone was soothing, reasonable, and firm.

"Yes, yes. However, I'm not sure everything in those boxes is a part of your study. There are notes in Richard's handwriting tucked among the packaged pottery. These may not all be your materials. His notes might help me figure out which is what."

"Hmm. Really? And you've been able to decipher what

the notes said?" Professor Faber's voice rose in a thin thread.

"Some. They appear to name small college museums and individuals, possibly collectors."

Professor Faber coughed into the phone. "Sorry, allergies," he said. After a moment, he continued. "That—that's wonderful. You have found our research materials. Those are the boxes I need back. They hold the artifacts Richard and I were working on. You've done a marvelous job identifying them."

"But I don't think I'm—"

"Thank you for all your work, Mrs. Watson. As I've said, you don't have to bother with them anymore. My research assistant will take over from here. Saturday, you said? He can bring his van and pick the cartons up that morning."

The last was a statement, not a suggestion. But since it was a timeline that Maggie had set in her own mind, she didn't argue.

"You really are amazingly conscientious," he went on. "I will be able to complete our project on time, just as Richard would have wanted."

"All the boxes with *SW* on them have been safely locked in the attic of my shop," she said. *No need to tell him about the break-ins.* "Have Conrad come to the shop at nine in the morning. My assistant can help him move them then."

She hung up the phone and sank onto a stool. Her throat constricted and her eyes burned. *As Richard would have wanted.* She hoped so, but the question of why Richard had never told her about this project with Professor Faber wouldn't let her go. Now she had only a couple of days to find out why he had those pots.

As the afternoon wore on, concerns over the Anasazi pottery and what it all meant tugged at her. On one hand, she couldn't wait to go through the notes and boxes again. On the other, she was afraid of what she might discover by doing so.

Troubling questions began rising to the surface. Would she

find that Richard was involved in some kind of illegal affair? Was Professor Faber involved as well, or was he the victim? The answers to these questions had the power to destroy her world.

Just as she thought things couldn't get worse, Conrad walked into the store. She hadn't seen him since the trip over to South Doe Island, and she hadn't missed him.

"I didn't expect to see you until Saturday," Maggie said. *And it's only Thursday.*

"I was touring the area. It's really nice around here. Good food too." He surveyed the store. June was in the back helping the only customer in at the moment. Eric was nowhere in sight.

"I'm glad you were able to get to know our town," Maggie said warmly. Maybe he wasn't so bad after all. "Where did you eat? Did you get to The Busy Bean?"

"I pick up breakfast there every morning. That Daisy is one talkative woman."

Maggie smiled. "Owning a café is perfect for her. She loves people."

"Yeah. I learned a lot about the town. And the people in it."

His words seemed simple enough, but, as so often was the case with Conrad, Maggie thought she sensed an undertone that wasn't quite friendly.

"For instance," Conrad continued, "she told me that while few people around here know much about First American pots, your employee, Eric, seems to know a lot. She'd heard he knew where to get some genuine pottery to sell if he found a buyer." He watched Maggie closely as he spoke.

Maggie laughed uneasily. "Eric is taking a class on American archaeology and he's very excited about it. He talks about it to everyone. It seems to be his new passion." She pursed her lips. "But he doesn't have anything to sell. Someone in the grapevine probably mixed that part up."

Maggie's mind pinged with images of Eric talking to the mint man about her having pottery that she might sell. Was Eric looking for buyers? Even the most trustworthy person could be tempted to cross the line when his need was great enough. How great were his father's financial problems?

"It's not unusual for him to be interested in Native American projectile points and pottery," Conrad said easily. "I do find it strange and quite a coincidence, however, that he's apparently even more interested in the marketing of such artifacts." He glanced at the stairs to the attic. "And you have quite a collection here." He let the implications of his statement hang unsaid between them.

Even though Maggie had her own doubts about Eric and his intentions, when Conrad all but accused him of being capable of stealing, she sprang to Eric's defense. "Eric is a fine young man. He's been in the Army and served his country." She looked Conrad up and down. "More than you can say. Plus, he's here in Somerset Harbor, caring for his sick father, when he could go live in the city, the way many young people his age do. And as for his job at the store, he's always shown himself to be honest, competent, and hardworking."

Conrad grinned at her. "If everything is on the up-and-up, why are you so upset?"

His attitude further infuriated her. He twisted everything around. *What is the matter with this guy? Why has he been so suspicious and hostile from the very beginning?* She bit her tongue to keep back her harsh reply.

Conrad peered at her, as if amused by her reaction. Then he looked at his watch. "Well, enough of this. I have to get back to Vermont. I have classes and appointments. I can't stay around here any longer. You've had several days to go through the boxes. Surely you've finished by now."

"I told you I'd be ready on Saturday," she said, straightening up on the stool. "And I just talked to Professor Faber, who agreed that you wouldn't come to get the boxes until then." She cast a quizzical look laced with irritation at him. "Didn't he tell you?"

Conrad's gray eyes seemed to take on an ominous look. "Stop messing around. Are you trying to hide something? I know what I'm supposed to get and what the boxes look like. You can't fool me."

Maggie started at his accusation. Hide something? Fool him? What was he talking about?

"Conrad, you're being ridiculous."

"Yeah? Then why all the delays?"

Exasperated at his continued belligerence, she threw up her hands. "Ask your professor about our Saturday agreement, if you don't believe me. Go ahead. Call him."

He shook his head. "Can't. He's out of the country. Had a meeting in Vienna."

Maggie stared at him. She'd just talked to the professor. How could Conrad lie like this?

"But you don't have to worry." Conrad now spoke as though talking to a child. "As I said, I know exactly what I'm supposed to bring back to the lab. I have a description of every piece of pottery." He accented the word *every* as if warning her.

"Hey, Maggie, I finished cleaning up those chests we brought over from South Doe Island," Eric called out as he approached the counter. Seeing the professor's assistant, he said, "Well, hi, Conrad. Good to see you."

Maggie was relieved to see Eric coming up, wiping his dirty hands on a rough rag and full of friendly good cheer.

Conrad didn't respond to Eric but addressed Maggie instead. "I'll be back Saturday morning to take those pots with me. Have them ready." He swung around and stomped out of the shop.

Eric gaped at the disappearing figure. "What's got into him?"

Maggie slumped back onto her stool, shaking her head. "He thinks I'm trying to pull something by not giving him the Anasazi pots right now. This whole thing is so confusing." She furrowed her brows. "If he weren't so difficult to deal with . . ." She sighed. "And he said Professor Faber was out of the country and not available. But I just talked to the professor this morning. Why would Conrad lie to me?" She drummed her fingers on the countertop. "Of course, even though Faber didn't mention being out of the country, I suppose he could still be. Maybe that's why he had to send Conrad to pick up his artifacts instead of coming himself."

Eric nodded. "Conrad probably didn't know Faber would be talking to you. He has an assignment: to bring Professor Faber's stuff back as soon as possible. He's probably just trying to push you into getting things done a little faster so he looks better to the professor."

She stared at the closed door. "Maybe. That's so manipulative." She massaged her temples. "I'm just glad he'll be gone soon. I don't believe I've ever met anyone that mercurial before."

18

After the shop closed, Maggie trudged up to the attic. It wasn't the obnoxious behavior of Professor Faber's assistant that dragged her heels. The problem that bothered her lay much closer to home.

It was the question of why Richard never said anything to her about these pots that hung over her like a bad dream.

Under the attic's glaring overhead lights, she took up the task of reexamining the SW boxes. As she did, she used her phone to systematically photograph each item, laying a ruler next to it to show its size. She didn't know why she bothered doing this, but it seemed right. Perhaps she was unwilling to let even these baffling items of Richard's go without a trace.

Halfway through the process, she paused and looked around her at the packing material, various pieces of pottery, and a few still-unopened boxes. She again wondered at her own compulsion to hold on to so much from the past. Shouldn't she let go? What was the purpose of taking all these pictures? She certainly wasn't going to look back over them. They were only inanimate objects. Nothing about her husband was in any of this.

Nevertheless, she opened the next box, took out its contents, laid the objects out on the floor, and carefully recorded each with her phone's camera.

After an hour, she'd gone through every cardboard box with SW emblazoned on its side. She now had a bunch of photos but no other information, no indication as to why Richard had these things.

She sighed deeply, drawing air into her lungs and slowly letting it out. The answer didn't lie in these boxes or in their notes. She had to admit she would probably never know it. And on Saturday, all of this would be taken away, back to Professor Faber's university lab.

She rose and took one last long, surveying gaze at the mounds of her husband's other containers lined up against the wall.

The light glanced off a clear, plastic container, catching her attention. She picked it up and turned it around. A black, three-inch-high *SW*, written on a white sheet of paper, had been placed inside, facing out.

She took the container to the center of the room where the lighting was best. Unlatching the top, she found a neatly organized set of manila file folders. Riffling through the folders, she read the labels on each tab. The files held old papers published by Professor Faber over the past twenty years, all before he'd been hired as a senior professor in Richard's department at the university. A casual examination revealed years of research of Southwestern art and pottery. If the number of papers published was any indication, the professor was certainly an expert in this area.

She placed the container with the *SW* cardboard boxes. She should send these reprints back to Professor Faber along with the pottery. She had no use for them. She started to snap the lid back in place but stopped. She took out the first file and flipped through it.

As she scanned the published paper, Maggie had the impression that many of the items mentioned in Faber's analysis were similar to those described in Richard's notes.

She began to reopen each *SW* cardboard box and to scrutinize her husband's handwritten notations. She sat under the glaring lights, comparing the pictures and museums mentioned in Professor Faber's papers with the pottery and cryptic notes found in the boxes.

After some time, she sat cross-legged on the floor and stared at the groupings of pottery around her. She rested her elbows on her knees and cupped her chin, thinking.

She consistently found that the most beautiful pots referred to in the paper overlapped with items on Richard's list.

Was Richard looking for something, some connection between Faber's professional papers and these boxes of priceless Anasazi pottery? Or was he working with Faber in the sale of these antiquities?

She closed her eyes. Did she really want an answer?

· · · · · · · · · · · · · · · · ·

Maggie invited her historical society friends over to Sedgwick Manor to give her an update on their research Friday morning. Ina and Ruth arrived together a little before nine with the treats from The Busy Bean they had offered to pick up. When Maggie opened the door to them, they greeted her jovially and bustled inside. Ruth carried a small stack of papers.

Maggie led them into the kitchen. Ruth dropped the papers onto the kitchen table and then took a seat beside Ina. Their bodies radiated restless energy. Maggie hurriedly put the kettle on and then joined them.

"Oh Maggie, we have such exciting news!" Ina burst out.

Ruth quickly stepped in. "We would have called you last night, but it was too late. This way, we can tell you everything at once."

"I can't wait to hear it." Maggie perched anxiously on the edge of her seat.

"Before, as you know, we matched those initials to colleges with museums," Ruth said.

"Our first step," Ina added, holding up a finger.

Ruth nodded. "But then we went further. Each of us actually contacted the museums and talked to either the curator or the museum's director. We each had a set of questions, general questions about the museums and their collection and more. We also asked some much more direct questions." She opened her eyes wide giving Maggie a meaningful look.

The doorbell rang again, just as the teakettle started singing.

"You get the door, I'll get the tea," Ina said, rising and going to the stove.

"Thanks," Maggie said, getting up. "Would you please take it and the treats to the dining room? I've already set out the cups."

At the front door, Liz, June, and Fran greeted Maggie with wide grins. James's mother came up the steps behind them. Deborah wasn't an official member of the historical society, but she helped them out occasionally. This morning, she appeared as eager as the others.

From all this palpable energy, Maggie was certain something major had been discovered. Her heart skipped a beat. She hoped that once her sleuthing friends told her their findings, she would be as delighted.

As the women settled around the large dining room table, Ruth and Ina joined them. Ina carried the pot of freshly brewed tea, and Ruth had the papers she'd brought along.

Once the teapot and plate of goodies made their rounds, Ruth cleared her throat. The others became quiet.

Ruth patted the pile of papers in front of her. "These are the notes that we took when we made those phone calls to the museums' curators and directors."

"I wanted to tape-record our phone calls too, for accuracy," Ina added, "but most of the contacts wanted our conversation to be off the record." She sniffed in frustration. "I may know shorthand, but it's not easy to take notes and talk at the same time. I'm worried I missed something."

"You did fine," Liz said with an encouraging smile. "We all were able to write down what was important."

"At first, I was really nervous about making those calls," Fran said, her ponytail swinging as she shook her head. "But people told us a lot, and they were so interesting."

"I think they trusted us because we said we were from the historical society," Deborah said. "If I'd just said 'Hi, I'm Deborah, and I have a bunch of personal questions to ask you about your organization and collection,' I don't think they'd have been as helpful."

Maggie smiled. "Are you going to tell me what you found out? Or just keep telling me what wonderful researchers you all are and make me guess?"

"Well," Ruth began, "the most important thing we found out is that—"

"Almost every one of the museums was missing several of their Anasazi and other prehistoric artifacts," Ina interrupted.

Ruth shot her an exasperated look.

Ina shrugged her shoulders. "Sorry. Guess I'm excited."

"We all are," Liz said. "But just think of that. Every one of them."

Maggie's head spun. She was dumbfounded for a few moments as she stared at her friends' faces, each one radiating joy at their success.

"These artifacts were missing? Were they reported as stolen or what?" Maggie asked.

"The two curators I talked to said they discovered the absences only recently," Fran said. "They were trying to get some pieces together to loan for an exhibition another museum was holding. The special exhibition was on Southwestern cultures and their art." She thoughtfully spread jam on her croissant. "Otherwise they still wouldn't know."

Maggie wondered fleetingly if the exhibit was being curated by the same museum borrowing pottery from Linda at the Coastal Maine Museum.

Deborah nodded in agreement with Fran. "That's pretty much what the museum director I talked to said happened. He'd gotten an e-mail about that same exhibition, wanting to see if their museum had any examples of early pottery to contribute. The director checked their records, ferreted out the boxes they were to be stored in, and found several of their best pieces missing."

"Same here," Ina said. "And worse—one of the museums I talked to said they found they had nothing but empty boxes. All of their Anasazi pots were gone."

Ruth clucked disapprovingly. "From what we can tell, none of the museums would even have known any of their collections were missing the Southwestern pottery if it hadn't been for that other museum asking around for pieces to show in their upcoming exhibition."

"Well, I guess that's natural," Liz said. "Who'd do an inventory of items in storage? They were cataloged and packed away. No reason to think they weren't still sitting on the shelf, tucked inside their boxes."

Maggie's throat constricted. She couldn't even drink a sip of tea. "When did they report their losses?"

"They didn't," Ina said. "None of the museums did. There're no official records of the theft of even one piece." She pursed her lips and pushed a tuft of white hair back under a hairpin.

Maggie shook her head. "I don't understand. Why weren't those thefts reported?"

"Well, first of all," Ruth said, "they had only recently discovered the items were missing and weren't done with their internal investigations yet. They also didn't report the losses because they wanted to avoid a scandal. They didn't want their donors or private collectors with pieces on loan to them to know. At least, not yet."

"Didn't want people to know?" Maggie said, incredulous.

"Apparently, that reaction isn't uncommon because several

of them said the same thing." Ruth flipped through the notes. "A couple of the directors added that they were afraid if the public knew, people would stop donating and loaning to the museum, because they wouldn't trust the museum to be able to protect the antiquities."

"Which appears to be an accurate assessment," Ina added.

"But weren't they searching for the culprit, the person who took them, so that they could get their collections back?" Maggie asked.

"Except for one or two museums, who were considering reporting their losses to the police and insurance company, all of the other directors and curators reminded us that if we had information leading to the materials, that they still belonged in the respective museums' collections," Ruth said. "From what we could gather, it looks like they are trying to figure this out 'in house,' each with their own methods, which they didn't share with us. It seems most of them only discovered their losses because of that curator requesting the pots for her special exhibition. I suppose the police and insurance companies will be their next step."

"So, how is it you all were able to get this secret information from them?" Maggie asked.

Slow grins of uncharacteristically smug smiles briefly appeared on each face as the women looked back at Maggie or, in Fran's case, down at her croissant.

"They only admitted it to us because, since we called them and asked about the pottery, they thought we already knew about their losses," Ruth explained.

"We were the ultimate undercover sleuths," Ina said.

The others laughed in shared enthusiasm.

Maggie had to agree that their research had led to a gold mine of information. Before she had a chance to congratulate them on their sleuthing, however, Ruth cleared her throat again.

"But that's not all," Ruth said. "The next bit of information we discovered was thanks to a suggestion from June. She was at the shop so she couldn't join the hunt, but she thought we should follow up on the collectors too."

"At first, we assumed the collectors were the donors, the ones who gave or loaned the Southwestern pottery to the museums," Ina said. "But then we realized that some of their collections were the result of archaeological digs sponsored by their parent university."

"As with the museums, we'd matched the initials to known collectors but hadn't contacted them directly," Ruth went on. "After calling all the museums, we ran down the collectors too."

"They proved to be a cagier group than the museum people were," Liz said, fiddling with the simple silver cross that hung around her neck. "They seemed more suspicious about who we were and why we were calling."

"Getting information from the guy I called was like pulling teeth," Fran said, then she smiled at Maggie. "But he finally answered my questions."

"You'll see when you read through these notes the specifics of each call," Ruth said. "These collectors weren't the donors. They were the buyers after the pieces left the museums. They each bought their particular Anasazi pottery pieces at different times over the years."

"The description of the guy who sold the pots to them—when they should have been in the museums' storage—sounds like the same person," Fran said.

"He told them he was from Utah and had inherited a collection from his father, who had just passed away. He wondered if the collector was interested in buying his pottery. He claimed his father had had the pots for years, ever since the seller was a boy." Ina sniffed. "All bogus, of course."

"In other words, they didn't know the antiquities had been taken from the various museum collections," Maggie said. She chewed her lower lip. "But they wouldn't tell you the name of the person they bought the pots from?"

The women shook their heads.

"And except for a rare e-mail, the seller contacted them by phone," Liz said. "So there's no trail."

"Okay, but then how did these pots end up in Richard's lab?" Maggie asked, afraid of the answer.

"That's where the story gets even more peculiar." Fran's normally quiet voice became more animated. "Apparently, the collectors were all contacted by a Dr. Watson, an archaeologist who was tracing down Southwestern antiquities for a study he was doing."

Maggie blanched. So what Faber claimed was true. He and Richard were working on a project together. *But why didn't I know anything about it? Why did Richard keep it a secret?*

"And they just sent their valuable antiquities to him?" Maggie asked. "Did they give a reason for such an unusual act?"

All of the women shook their heads or raised their shoulders in response. "None of them told us why, just that they did it," Ruth said, giving her a wide-eyed look. "It seemed highly unusual to us too."

The group continued their discussion, elaborating on their findings as they enjoyed tea and treats.

Maggie noticed that Ina had become unusually quiet. The older lady took a bite of her muffin but seemed lost in thought.

When the group was leaving, Ina lagged behind. At the door, with the others already down the walkway, Ina invited Maggie to come over to her house for lunch.

"I want to share a loaf of French bread I've just baked," Ina said. "You've got to check out this magical new baking technique I've learned from an Internet video. With your interest in homemade bread, you'll definitely want to try it."

Maggie agreed to come over and they set a time.

Still in emotional turmoil over her friends' successful sleuthing,

Maggie digested the morning's revelations. These new findings pushed against her sense of comfort, of her security in believing she knew her life with Richard. *Was the man I respect and love involved in something illegal? Or was he really working with Dr. Faber? But if so, what were they doing?*

Part of her wished she'd never opened up that first container—it had been a Pandora's box from the start.

19

Troubled and thoughtful after her friends left, Maggie took her time cleaning up the kitchen before heading out to run some errands. As she put away the last dish, her cell phone rang. She looked around the room, but it was nowhere in sight. She heard it again. She hurried into the hallway and found it sitting next to a crystal vase of daffodils on the Hapsburg console table. Glancing at the flowers as she picked up the phone, she considered getting some to take to Ina when she went over for lunch.

Maggie caught the call just in time before it went to voice mail.

"Hi, Maggie." James's warm voice made her smile. "Just checking to see how you're doing and if you can get together for lunch. Daisy's special today is a fish sandwich with homemade chips."

Maggie started walking back to the kitchen. "I'd love to, but Ina invited me over."

"Ah, you're one popular lady," he said, his cheerful voice betraying slight disappointment.

"I'm glad you called though," she said, taking a seat in the bright breakfast nook. "The historical society members—including your mom, by the way—did a bit of research for me about some notes I found in Richard's boxes. Did Deborah tell you anything about it?"

"Nope. She probably thought it was private since it was a special request from you. She wouldn't mention anything without your okay, even to me. What did they find out? Something of interest?"

"You could say that." Maggie filled him in on their findings.

James let out a low whistle. "Missing antiquities were stolen from museums, were sold to collectors, and then ended up in your husband's possession. You say there's no real information on the seller? No way to trace him down?"

"There doesn't seem to be. All of the communication between him and the buyers was over the phone. One of the latest sales had a couple of e-mail messages, but the buyer had deleted that long ago. Not to mention the fact that he's since replaced that computer and can't remember what he did with the old one." She grimaced at how convenient that was for the buyer. No trace of him or the seller. "And nobody would say how the money and pottery were exchanged."

"Yet these collectors just sent them off to Richard? They were willing to send their valuable prehistoric pots to someone who simply contacted them and said he wanted to examine them as part of an archaeological study?" James sounded incredulous.

"I know. It sounded incredible to us too. But that's apparently what they did, or what they all claimed they did, anyway. The pots were insured, of course, but money couldn't replace owning them."

"And to a true collector, ownership is everything," James said.

Maggie shifted uncomfortably on the chair.

"Something's missing. Collectors are investors too, in a way," he continued. "These men probably valued their Southwestern collections for the objects themselves, but I bet they also valued them for their monetary worth. Whether they knew it or not at the time, it appears they all bought their pots from the black market."

Maggie nodded to the empty space around her.

"Did the women say if Richard used e-mail to request the pottery?" James asked.

"They didn't ask specifically. If he did, there'd be a paper trail, so to speak." Maggie didn't feel particularly optimistic.

James seemed to pick up on her tone. "Listen, Maggie. From

everything you've told me about your husband, he was a good man. I don't think he'd suddenly be involved in something illegal at that stage of his life. There's got to be a good explanation for all of this."

Maggie closed her eyes. Images of Richard materialized in her internal vision: working in his lab, typing reports, teaching students, sharing stories with her.

"And yet, here are all these apparently stolen Anasazi artifacts, sent to him from a bunch of different collectors," she said.

"Professor Faber told you they were working on something together. Maybe he can explain it."

"Perhaps. But then why didn't he say something yesterday when I told him about finding Richard's notes?"

"They may have been investigating something that he didn't want to involve you in. Didn't you say you found a warning note written by your husband?"

"Yes."

"Did you tell the police about it?" he asked.

"Um . . ."

"Maggie, they need to know. Look at all the strange things that have been happening. They may not be connected, but I'm beginning to think they probably are."

Maggie frowned. James might be right, but she didn't want to involve the police in this. They couldn't do anything about an old note stuck in an envelope. There'd been no crime that she knew of, and nothing to indicate what the threat referred to. Richard had died of an aortic aneurysm, not murder. Not to mention that the note was now several years old.

She forced a laugh. "You worry too much. With the uptick in people coming through town now that it's spring, those break-ins probably really were crimes of opportunity." Before James could argue, she quickly went on. "But you're undoubtedly right about Faber. I'll ask him about all of this later. Maybe Conrad knows something too. I'll be seeing him tomorrow when he picks up the boxes."

Maggie had just hung up the phone when it rang again. A friendly yet professional voice came over the line.

"Hi, Maggie, it's Linda from the Coastal Maine Museum. I found some information you might be interested in regarding insurance values and recent sales prices for prehistoric First American artifacts, as well as other information on the buyers and sellers."

Maggie was delighted that the museum curator had followed up on her questions about the Southwestern pottery.

"That's wonderful," Maggie said. "I have a lunch date, but I can come over right now if that's okay with you. I took pictures of every piece I'm interested in with my phone. I'll show them to you when I come."

"Sounds good. I'll see you shortly."

Maggie drove over to the museum and parked in its lot. A young volunteer at the desk directed her to Linda's office.

The door was open. Maggie stuck her head in and tapped on the doorjamb.

Linda looked up from her computer and gestured to a chair in front of her ample oak desk. "Come in, come in."

Linda's office was much like her—warm yet professional. The familiar smell of books intermingling with a slightly spicy fragrance immediately made Maggie feel comfortable. Filing cabinets, bookshelves, and freestanding wooden cabinets lined two walls. Near a window, a small table holding a potted fern was flanked by two floral upholstered chairs. Linda's desk dominated the adjacent wall, facing the door.

"Thank you for meeting with me so quickly," Maggie said, pulling up a chair in front of Linda's desk.

"I'm glad you could come so soon. This won't take long. I

know you've got somewhere to be."

While Linda was talking, her phone rang. She glanced at the screen. "Sorry, I have to get this," she said, then answered the call. After listening, she murmured, "Okay, I'll be there," and hung up.

"Everything okay?" Maggie asked.

"An unexpected meeting has come up, but we have a few minutes. And you can take the papers showing the information I've found with you. May I see the pictures you took?"

Maggie immediately pulled out her phone. Finding the photographs she'd taken of the Anasazi pottery, she handed her phone over to the curator.

Linda's eyes widened as she scrolled through the pictures. After a few minutes, she looked up at Maggie. "These are amazing. If they are the real thing and not reproductions, they cover quite a number of pottery periods and types within the Anasazi tradition." She laid the phone on her desk. "Where did you say these are from?"

"They're part of a research project a professor in Vermont is carrying out," Maggie said, hedging slightly.

"How did he or she manage to amass so many in one place? As I understand it, usually people have to travel to museums to study such antiquities." Linda pressed her lips together. "At least that's been my experience."

"These were all in the hands of private collectors," Maggie said. "Not museums."

Linda nodded and looked through the pictures once more. Her interest in the pictures was obvious. "They're so beautiful. So rare." She looked up at Maggie. "That professor must be quite convincing to get private collectors to send their pots to him." She smiled. "I'd like him to work for me. I'd be able to put together some amazing exhibitions with someone who has that skill."

"He's been in the field for many years, so I guess he knows a lot of people. That's probably why he has been so successful at getting these things."

Linda perked up. "Who is it? I used to know the literature in this area quite well."

"Professor Faber. Daniel Faber."

"Oh yes. I've read several of his papers. Years ago." She looked at the picture of a shallow bowl with a black geometric design painted on its sides. "That would explain it."

"Do you know him?"

"No. I've never met him. But his name is quite familiar."

Maggie didn't know if she should feel relieved or more perplexed. Richard's involvement was still unexplained.

"Are you doing research for him?" Linda asked Maggie.

"Not exactly."

"Mm-hm. But you have the pottery here? In Somerset Harbor?" Linda asked quizzically.

"Well, it's a weird story," Maggie said. "Before he passed away, my husband was working with Professor Faber. Somehow, the university, thinking the boxes of artifacts were Richard's, sent all of these pots to me. The mistake was only recently discovered."

"Oh, how terrible." Linda tapped the desk near Maggie's phone. "And you didn't realize it earlier?"

"No. I thought the boxes were Richard's personal field materials. I had no reason to go through them, and it would have been too painful for me."

"To think that these priceless heirlooms could have been lost through such a slip." Linda shook her head. "It just goes to show how we must be careful in even the most mundane tasks."

"It certainly does."

The curator pushed back in her chair. "I wish we had more time," Linda said, clearly reluctant to tear herself away from the images. She opened a desk drawer and withdrew a red folder. Placing it on the desk, she opened it and turned it toward Maggie.

"Here's a list of the Southwestern pottery I was able to trace, giving their insurance values and recent auction sales." Linda folded her hands. "This is all unofficial, of course. As a representative of the museum, I cannot comment on objects' values. Please keep this information confidential. And please don't let anyone know I gave it to you."

"Thank you for doing this. I owe you one."

Maggie leaned over the folder. There were two columns. In the left column were images of various pieces of pottery, which Maggie could now recognize as Southwestern. The pots were clustered together by time period. Under each image there was a specific cultural name and the years the pieces were produced. On the right, next to each image, was a description of the piece and its provenance, insurance value, and last auction sale price.

"As you can see, the collection you have is worth a small fortune." She gazed at Maggie. "You must be very careful in repacking them. It would be a tragedy if any of them were broken or chipped in shipping them back to the professor."

At this admonition, a small smile tugged at Maggie's lips. "I'll be very careful. And they won't be shipped through the mail. Professor Faber's assistant is going to drive them back to Vermont. They'll be quite safe." Safe from damage, but she wondered if she was doing the right thing by sending them back to Faber. Was he—and was Richard, when he was alive—working privately on behalf of the museums in returning the stolen antiquities? Was the academic research scenario just a ruse in order to keep the thefts out of the public eye? She hoped so.

Glancing at the wall clock, Linda said, "I wish I could stay longer, but take these papers with you. They will give you an idea of what those pots you have might be worth. Of course, the market always changes, but it's a good indication of your collection's value. The professor is probably already aware of these figures. If he's doing a research project, I'm sure the university had to get insurance to cover any loss or damage to these artifacts."

Linda stood up and handed the folder and phone to Maggie.

"If you're still interested and you'd like to know more about Southwestern pottery," the curator said, "we can set up another time to discuss it."

Maggie thanked her and left the museum. With the help of her historical society friends and Linda, she was developing a more complete picture of those Southwestern pots, although she still wasn't sure what they meant exactly. However, she felt she was getting closer to the answer. She tossed the folder onto the back seat of her car, hopped in, and pulled away from the curb.

On the way to Ina's, Maggie checked her watch, noting she had just enough time to stop at the florist. She pulled into a free parking spot on a side street just around the corner from the shop.

Bright blue barrels of spring flowers called to her as soon as she entered The Singing Mermaid Floral Shoppe. An almost overpowering fragrance accosted her. With so many flowers in the small, warm space, their competing scents took a moment to adjust to.

Maggie delighted at the daffodils, tulips, roses, and other specialty flowers. It didn't take her long to choose a bouquet of white narcissus with sunny yellow centers. These were the flowers that most reminded her of her spring garden in Vermont.

There were no other customers in the store. Behind the counter, one of the shop's florists, Anne Baker, was tying ribbon into bows at a worktable covered in foot-high vases. Maggie suspected preparations were underway for a weekend wedding celebration.

"All set?" Anne asked.

"Yep, just these today," Maggie said.

"Do you want me to add a ribbon?"

"Sure. Thanks, Anne."

As Anne tied a ribbon around Maggie's bouquet, she remarked on the success of the first History by Candlelight Tour. "James really came up with a great idea," she said. "He did a good job advertising it too. I could tell that we had more tourists coming into town earlier this year than before."

Maggie agreed. "June and I definitely noticed better numbers and more people coming through the last couple weeks."

"He's got a lot of good ideas for building our town's economy." The young woman's eyes widened in admiration. "My mom says he's the most proactive alderman we've had in years."

Maggie felt a tug of pleasure at the woman's enthusiasm for James and his work. After chatting a few more minutes, Maggie paid for the flowers and left with them tucked in the crook of her arm.

The fresh, clean coastal air filled her lungs and she strode swiftly around the corner. She didn't want to be late for lunch with Ina.

As she removed her keys from her purse, she glanced at the Jetta. She halted abruptly, almost dropping the keys and her pretty bouquet.

The rear driver's-side window was smashed, and the door was slightly ajar. She peered in through a hole in the shattered glass.

Linda's folder was gone.

Furious, Maggie called the police. As soon as she said hello, the receptionist, Paula Ellis, said, "Don't tell me you have another problem, Maggie."

Maggie couldn't tell if Paula was being sympathetic, sarcastic, or funny, none of which was welcome. She'd been calling the police so frequently, she didn't even have to identify herself. Paula recognized her phone number.

"I'm sorry to hear that," Paula said after Maggie told her what had happened. "Around the corner from The Singing Mermaid, you said? Someone will be there soon."

Maggie had just finished going through her glove box to make sure nothing else was taken when a squad car pulled up behind her. Robert Linton got out, his face dour.

At least he didn't have his lights flashing. All I need is more attention. Not that the whole community wouldn't know about it within the hour anyway. Ina's trusty police scanner always seemed to come into play in these situations.

It didn't take Officer Linton long to size up the situation, ask questions, and take notes.

"This is pretty unusual," he said. "We rarely have smash-and-grab incidents, and never at this time of the day." He looked down at Maggie. "And you say the only thing missing is a file folder?"

"It was on the seat. Nothing's missing from my glove box." She looked at the front seats once more and scowled. "No. That's all. Just the file."

"Any idea why someone would break your window to steal a file folder? What was in it?"

"Just some notes about sale prices of antiques," she said. "Nothing valuable."

"And there wasn't anything of value lying around that would have incited someone to break into your car?"

"Nothing."

"I'll get fingerprints on the door and handle, but it's not likely we'll find the culprits. In today's world, every criminal knows to avoid leaving fingerprints, and there wasn't really anything to fence." Officer Linton tapped his pencil on his notepad and looked down the street. "Of course, it's pretty quiet here."

"I know, I know, it could have been another crime of opportunity," she said, unable to keep the exasperation out of her voice. "Don't you think I've been having more than my share of 'crimes of opportunity'?"

"I understand your frustration, but we can only go on evidence. I would guess this was an unfortunate incidence of vandalism, and you just happened to be in the wrong place at the wrong time. Maybe they just took the folder to inconvenience you. Do you have any idea why someone might want to vandalize your property?"

She shook her head. "No good ideas."

"I'm sorry I can't do more." The officer jabbed his small notebook and pen into his chest pocket and, after a kindly reminder to call if she had any more problems, left.

Not wanting to disappoint Ina by canceling lunch, Maggie called the garage to see if they could repair her window later that day. Kat Auld answered briskly. "Auld's Automotive. May I help you?"

Maggie quickly laid out her dilemma.

"No problem. Bob should be able to get a window for your

car and have the old one replaced by this afternoon if you get it here right away. We'll give you a loaner."

Relieved, Maggie drove directly over to Auld's, left her car in their care, and walked out to the loaner Buick parked in front of the old building. As she started the engine, a rap on the passenger's window made her jump.

The couple from South Carolina who had been in the shop last week were peering in at her, grinning.

Maggie opened the window. "Well, how nice to see you," she said, hiding her confusion as to why they'd stopped her.

"We're so glad we caught you before we left town," the husband said. "We wanted to tell you how much we enjoyed seeing your antiques shop and going to the History by Candlelight Tour."

"I'm happy to hear it."

He continued. "We're about to begin a new antiques business back home, and you've given us some great inspiration as we establish our shop in our own little historical town."

The wife nodded enthusiastically. "This trip has been wonderful."

"Well, we'd best be going," her husband said. "Just wanted to say thanks."

With that, they waved goodbye and sauntered down the street, the wife talking with great animation, her hands flying as if drawing plans in the air.

As Maggie watched them leave, she felt a glow. They admired her shop and her town, two things of great importance to her. As she swung out of the parking space and drove away, a sense of fulfillment replaced the aggravation she'd been nurturing since finding her car broken into.

In spite of everything, she managed to arrive at Ina's house within minutes of their agreed-upon time.

Ina greeted her at the door wearing a white chef's coat.

"Perfect timing," she said. "I just finished up in the kitchen."

Maggie entered and followed Ina through the hall and into the dining room. Three place settings of Royal Albert china and crystal glasses had been carefully laid out on the table.

Following Maggie's glance toward the table, Ina said, "I also invited Connie for lunch. She seems like such a nice young girl."

The doorbell rang, and Ina retraced her steps to the front door. She returned with Connie in tow. On seeing Maggie, the young woman cast a sidelong glance at Ina, then greeted her quietly.

"I almost didn't recognize you without a camera at your eye," Maggie joked, puzzled by Connie's somewhat reserved behavior.

"It's my signature look," Connie said with an obliging smile. She stepped over to one of the dining chairs and placed her purse on the floor near it.

Ina had already laid lunch out on the table. A leafy Greek salad speckled with Kalamata olives and chunks of tomato, cucumber, and feta cheese filled a large porcelain bowl, and a perfectly golden loaf of bread graced a wooden board.

"Is that the famous bread you were telling me about?" Maggie asked.

"Fresh out of the oven," Ina said proudly.

As they made small talk, Maggie wondered if Ina was going to mention her car incident. However, the topic never came up. Apparently, the wily purveyor of justice hadn't been listening to her police scanner.

"You girls take your seats," Ina said. As they did what she asked, she cut into the crusty bread with a satisfying crunch, then handed out slices.

After a bite, Maggie opened her eyes wide in appreciation. "I'll definitely want to learn how to make this," she said. "It's just as you said—beautiful crust on the outside and chewy on the inside. Wonderful texture."

Ina danced in her chair. "And you'll love how easy it is to make."

The lunch passed in friendly banter with remarks on food and baking, the history behind the Royal Albert china, and, of course, town happenings and local family histories. Nevertheless, Maggie couldn't help but notice that Connie seemed nervous. She talked incessantly throughout the lunch, slipping from one topic to another and back again.

Over butter pecan ice cream, Maggie brought the conversation back to the bread, which she thought was the reason Ina had invited her over.

"Oh, let me show you the critical baking tool for it," Ina said. She jumped up, scuttled into the kitchen, and returned bearing a cast-iron Dutch oven, which she set on the table in front of Maggie. "I was surfing the cooking sites when I saw something on a no-knead French bread. I went to the video and the rest is history. It was as easy as can be."

All during Ina's explanation, Connie fiddled with her crystal water glass, pushing it around on the table. Her eyes followed the rainbows that danced over the cloth's embroidered flowers when the chandelier's light turned the glass into a prism.

Acknowledging at last how anxious Connie was behaving, Ina stopped and gave the young woman a significant glance.

Connie swallowed and unceremoniously blurted out, "I've got something to tell you." She turned squarely to face Maggie. Her fingers quivered as she reached for her water glass once more. "I . . . I . . . that is—"

"It's all right, Connie," Ina said. "Spit it out."

Maggie looked from one to the other, mystified.

"I'm sorry, but I took a necklace from your pirate chest," Connie blurted.

Maggie stared at her. *What?*

"I took the pearl-and-pendant necklace. I didn't mean to steal it."

Ina scowled at her.

Connie looked away. "Well, I did mean to, I guess, but I replaced it with a long string of faux pearls. You thought it was costume jewelry anyway, so I didn't think it would hurt." She glanced at Ina's stern expression and then at Maggie.

"I know it was wrong. I shouldn't be trying to justify what I did." She stared down at her glass. "After I took the necklace, I couldn't get over deceiving you."

Maggie gaped at the reporter. How could exchanging one bauble with another cause so much guilt? Something was missing in this story. She shot a questioning glance at Ina.

Ina patted Connie's hand. "Let me explain." She smiled at Maggie. "Connie and I got to talking, and she told me everything."

Ina then launched into a long and convoluted story about Connie's grandmother and how, some years ago, a devastating fire had wiped out her entire home. The only thing the family had been able to save was a small case holding a picture of Connie's great-grandfather and great-grandmother on their wedding day and the necklace she was wearing in the photo—a strand of pearls that had a ruby-and-diamond encrusted pendant.

Ina paused and gestured at Connie to tell Maggie the rest.

Connie remained silent, her cheeks a bright red and her eyes on a teaspoon she turned over and over in her hand.

"The necklace was passed to one of Connie's aunts," Ina said, picking up the story as Connie faltered. "When the aunt died, her daughter found it. The daughter didn't know anything of the necklace's history. It looked like an ostentatious piece of costume jewelry to her. She didn't know much about gems, anyway. The only valuable jewelry she had was her wedding ring with its small diamond. So she threw the necklace into a shoe box full of other costume jewelry and sold it at her garage sale."

"How did Connie recognize it?" Maggie asked. Then, realizing she was talking about Connie who sat in front of her, she rephrased the question. Turning to Connie, she said, "How did you recognize it as your great-grandmother's? Maybe you're wrong about it and it really is costume jewelry after all."

Connie shook her head. "I have a large framed picture of her in my living room. And she's wearing the necklace. But I didn't know what had happened to my family's heirloom until I saw it in that photo you showed me at the historical society meeting of it dangling out of the pirate chest. I recognized it immediately."

Maggie opened her mouth to speak, then closed it again.

Connie continued. "The necklace is worth thousands of dollars. But as a link to my family, it is priceless to me. When I saw it, I realized immediately that I could never afford to buy it for its true value." She bowed her head for a moment, then looked up at Maggie. "I'm still paying my school debts, and I've just started working. There's no way I could come up with that much money."

Everyone was silent for a few moments, digesting what Connie had just said, before she continued.

"I went to the shop every day just to see the necklace. Then one day I realized that because you had the necklace casually draped out of the chest and onto the floor, completely unprotected, clearly you had no idea the pearls and jewels were real. As far as you or anyone knew, it was just another fake bauble." Connie folded and unfolded a corner of her napkin. "So I replaced it with a piece of costume jewelry." She looked down at her hands.

Ina and Maggie exchanged glances.

"I'm so sorry." Connie's voice broke. "I regret that I ever took it. I've never done anything like that before, but I couldn't bear to see my great-grandmother's wedding necklace like that, just tossed in with a bunch of fakes. At the same time, I couldn't tell you what it was because that would put it way beyond my ability to buy it." She stopped and started again. "Afterward, I couldn't look at the necklace without thinking how ashamed of me my great-grandmother would be. I'd stolen, even with good intentions."

Tearfully, Connie reached down into her purse and brought out the dazzling string of pearls and pendant. The chandelier's light bounced off the diamond and ruby facets, creating a play of light. She reached across the table and laid it in front of Maggie.

As Maggie tried to wrap her head around this strange tale, she gently picked up the necklace and let it drape through her fingers. She studied it. The chandelier continued to throw its flashes of color around the room. How did she ever think this was a glass bauble? She stroked the pearled strands, then handed it back to Connie.

"I bought this for five dollars. To me, it is a prop. To you, it is your heritage, a part of your family. You should keep it."

Tears welled up in Connie's eyes. She stared at her family's legacy. With a slow, thoughtful sigh, the young woman shook her head. "It was my great-grandmother's, but it was never rightfully mine. I was wrong to believe it was."

The three sat discussing who owned what, when, where, and why. After some time, Maggie and Connie, with judicious input from Ina, agreed the best thing would be to give the necklace on permanent loan to the Somerset Harbor Historical Society Museum. Connie's ancestors were among the founding citizens of the town. In this way, the necklace would always be a memorial to Connie's family tree.

"And," Ina added with a grin, "it'll never end up in a garage sale again."

That evening, Maggie stood in her kitchen ruminating about the strange events of the day. Nearby, Snickers played with his toy mouse, entertaining her with his hunting antics.

Maggie removed a loaf of sourdough from the oven and placed it on a rack to cool. She loved to bake. The time-honored tradition had always soothed her. It gave her an opportunity to step back from all the crazy things that had been happening—and they did seem to be crazy—and relax while her subconscious worked on processing recent events and her conscious focused on making something.

As she walked past the counter, she patted her newly discovered Dutch oven. After returning from Ina's lunch, she'd scoured her aunt's storage area, sure that she'd seen one similar to Ina's in the midst of organizing Richard's boxes. Sure enough, she found a close match on a shelf in the attic. Tomorrow, she'd try Ina's French bread baking technique.

Tonight, however, she'd have fresh sourdough with carrot soup and a salad. She dished up her meal and brought it to the breakfast table. Just as she sat down to eat, the phone rang and James's familiar voice greeted her.

It had only been a short time since she'd talked to him, but so much had happened. She began by filling him in about her meeting with the museum's curator. They speculated on what it all meant: the antiquities' value, Faber's expertise in the area but not Richard's, and Richard's mysterious notes.

Finally, James said, "It looks to me like Richard and Professor

Faber had discovered a collection of stolen prehistoric artifacts. Perhaps they intended to return them to their appropriate museums but hadn't yet."

Maggie didn't agree. "There are a couple of problems with that. First, there's the mailing label on each box. Those pots were sent directly to Richard, not to Faber, and they came from the collectors. From what the historical society ladies found out, the museums don't know where their materials are. As far as they're concerned, their pieces are still missing."

She choked back the rising kernel of doubt that had been threatening to overwhelm her and went on. "I don't believe Richard would ever withhold such information from them without good reason. But maybe he died before he was able to share his findings."

"Maybe." James sounded dubious.

Maggie blew out a puff of air, as if to release the frustration building up in her. "And then there are the collectors. They all claim they only bought pots legally. None of them indicated in any way that they expected to have their precious pots returned to the museums. I don't believe they would have agreed to send them to Richard if they thought they'd lose them."

"Then why did they send him their collections?"

"That's something we don't know. None of the collectors said why Richard wanted the pots or why they agreed to send them." She stared down at her hand. "I just don't believe Richard would have kept stolen antiquities. Not if he knew they were stolen."

"Apparently, he did." James's tone was patient but unrelenting. "Maybe he wanted to examine them in more detail first. Once finished, it's possible the pieces would go to their designated museums."

Maggie shook her head. "I just don't see him doing that. Not even to be able to further his own research and career by carrying out an analytical study of these rare antiquities. He would certainly have contacted the museums and informed them of his finds."

"I don't know what he was thinking," James said, "but from everything you've told me so far, Richard's notes clearly show that he knew which museums the stolen antiquities had come from. He discovered the collectors who bought them and somehow managed to get them to send him the stolen pots. At the same time, there is no indication he contacted any of the museums about his findings."

Words caught in Maggie's throat. The implication of what James had said troubled her greatly and poked at that doubt lurking in the back of her mind. She couldn't speak.

James continued. "I'm not saying Richard intended to do anything illegal himself, just that he hadn't contacted them yet."

Maggie's mind whirled. She felt that word "yet" implied more than James wanted to say out loud. Did he believe her husband had intended to keep this cache of valuable antiquities? How could James even suggest Richard wasn't honest? She wanted to slam down the phone.

Instead, she said, "What about the note Richard wrote saying he was worried about our safety? He believed there was danger in this." She couldn't keep the edge out of her voice.

"Maggie, I'm sorry. I wasn't saying that Richard did anything wrong. But we do have to look at all the possible angles, even if we don't yet understand the reasoning behind them. I'm sure we just don't have all the information yet."

Maggie was mollified but still wanted to cut the rest of their phone call short. She needed time to absorb the new possibilities and where they might lead.

She sat gazing out the window at the streetlights pushing away the darkness. Her soup was getting cold. This phone call had gone on too long—it had become unpleasant, uncomfortable. She was aware of James saying something, but she'd stopped listening.

As she continued to concentrate on the nighttime shadows, a brief spot of light caught her attention. She straightened up and strained to peer out the window more closely. The unfamiliar light came from the carriage house.

"Oh no," she muttered. "Not again."

"What? What's wrong?" James asked.

"I think my would-be thief has returned to the scene of the crime," Maggie growled.

"Call the police. I'm coming right over."

"No, don't bother. At this point, I'm sure it's Eric. I can see his car there on the road. Not a great thief, is he? I'll call you after I take care of things." She hung up the phone.

Maggie didn't want Eric to get into real trouble, which he would if she called the police. She wanted to shake him. This was not the way to get out of a financial problem. If she caught him in the act, it would show him how easily his whole life could be ruined by this foolish attempt at stealing.

She pulled Ina's heavy flashlight out of a kitchen drawer and marched out the door.

22

Maggie found the carriage house door open. With a cursory glance, she could tell the lock had been jimmied. Slowly pushing the door open, she stepped from the moonlit night into the shop's greater darkness. She held her flashlight in front of her but didn't turn it on. Once inside, she closed the door and stood still, listening for footsteps.

She planned on surprising Eric for maximum shock value. Just when he was confidently rummaging through things, thinking no one knew, Maggie would stun him by turning on her light. In the shop's murky gloom, Maggie realized that using the literal light could also be a metaphor for showing him the figurative light.

Within a few moments that felt like hours, she heard heavy, hesitant steps coming down the stairs. There was just enough difference in light between the outside and inside that her form would be silhouetted against the door's leaded glass window, so she stepped to the side wall. Now she merged with the darkness.

A faint light appeared, erratically searching out each step as a pair of well-polished men's shoes carefully followed the glow. Maggie held her breath—it sounded too loud in the store's stillness. The creak of each stair as the intruder made his way down warned he was coming closer. When he was halfway down the steps, she turned her flashlight on and aimed it at his face.

"What the . . . ?" Squinting, a thin, pasty-faced man carrying a medium cardboard box with a black *SW* twisted awkwardly away from the intense light.

Maggie gaped momentarily, staring. Her light didn't expose

a young Eric on her steps, but a middle-aged man with thinning hair wearing a tan jacket.

It was the mint man.

Maggie quickly recovered from the shock at not finding her shop assistant. All the sightings she'd had of this peppermint-loving man over the past several days flashed through her mind. In the shop, at the garage sale, in Daisy's restaurant. Sometimes wearing a long overcoat, sometimes this tan jacket.

She stepped forward, keeping her light directly in his eyes. "My thoughts exactly," she said drily.

She swept her light across the store's floor. Two other cardboard boxes sat at the bottom of the stairs. Both had *SW* on their sides. She flashed the beam back to the mint man, reached over to the wall on her right, and flipped on the store's lights. The room lit up, as bright as day.

The man's surprised expression quickly dissolved. He slowly continued down the stairs.

"Don't get excited," he said, his voice cool and solicitous. "This box is heavy and, as you know, its contents are precious. I am merely going to put it down."

Maggie's mind raced. *What should I do now?*

"I suppose you saw my light. Couldn't be helped. The streetlights coming through the windows weren't enough for me to see by. I had to use a flashlight. Such a shame. This is the second time its light has given me away."

Once he reached the base of the steps, he placed the box in his arms on top of one of the others, aligning them so that they wouldn't tip and fall over. He patted the box, straightened up, and rested his hand on top of the small pile.

Maggie swallowed hard. "You're Professor Faber, aren't you?" *I guess that car outside isn't Eric's.*

He smirked. "How did you know it was me?"

"I didn't at first. I suspected my assistant."

"Ah, yes. Your little friend, Eric. He has quite an appetite for these beauties himself, doesn't he? He would be a logical culprit." Faber looked as if he were playing a scenario through his mind. "Yes, he'd be a good candidate. But what about Conrad? You didn't suspect him?"

Unmoored by this strange situation, Maggie figured her best option was to play along and keep up her end of the conversation.

"Yes, I also suspected Conrad for a while. You told me you had given him exact descriptions of which boxes held the Southwestern pottery. It'd be easy for him to quickly remove only the important containers, leaving the others untouched."

"Of course. I wanted him to know as much as possible for a couple of reasons."

"You tried to persuade me to let him take the boxes without my searching through them. Without finding Richard's notes."

Faber snorted with disgust. "Richard. He was such a diligent, boring, cross-every-T sort of researcher. I was sure he had notes somewhere. And I guessed he would keep them with the artifacts. But I needed those boxes."

"So you sent Conrad," Maggie said.

Faber's steely eyes settled on Maggie. "I had primed him. He could have easily identified the boxes. If he ever had the chance to search for them. But you never let him. I kind of expected that. Hoped for it, really. You played right into my scheme." He oozed smugness.

Maggie wondered what he was referring to but didn't want him to see her uncertainty.

He eyed her closely. "But how did you recognize me, I wonder? I could be any thief prowling through your place. We've never met face-to-face, and I wasn't supposed to be here in Somerset Harbor."

Common thieves don't wear wingtips. "Well, neither Eric nor Conrad is sneaking down my stairs, stealing the Anasazi pots. You are. And who else would know exactly which boxes held the valuable artifacts?"

He bowed. "Not bad." He grinned, but there was no warmth in his expression.

Professor Faber nonchalantly continued bragging about how he had deceived her. How he had followed her in order to discover if she was contacting anyone else about the pottery. How he had trailed her to the museum earlier that day, where he saw her bring out the bright red folder.

Maggie idly wondered if she could keep him talking until June showed up for work the next morning. Given how pleased he seemed to be with himself, it might work.

"I had to find out what was in the file," he continued. "That's why I broke into your car. Your stop for flowers proved to be the perfect opportunity."

He gloated about his chatting up Eric in the shop. "He was so eager to tell me all about your husband's things. He even took me into the storage room and showed me around. When we were in there, I saw the keys to the attic hanging from a hook over the worktable."

"But why are you trying to steal these Anasazi pots? Your assistant was going to come tomorrow to pick them up anyway."

"Come now, don't you know?"

It clicked. "You wanted to set up a scenario that made it look like they were stolen, so that no one would even consider you were involved. It was a plan of misdirection. No one would try to trace the theft back to you . . . you, the original thief."

He broke out in a loud guffaw. "Impressive deduction."

"So Conrad was just another patsy. He had no idea you intended to steal these valuable antiquities. He was a part of your alibi. Your trusting student, ready to speak up for your passion about protecting First American heritage."

"Those most committed to a cause are often the most easily deceived. All I had to do to cement Conrad's opinion of me was to talk continually about how terrible pothunters were and how collectors were aiding and abetting the massive destruction of archaeological sites, causing the loss of scientific knowledge. He saw me as the righteous warrior fighting against evil."

"All the while you were stealing pots from museums where you had access to the collections because of your legitimate career, then selling them to collectors who would never expose you because they wanted those pots for themselves."

A self-satisfied grin spread over the professor's face. "It was a beautiful plan, if I may say so myself."

"But then, why would they have sent the pots to Richard if they had them tucked away in their own collections?"

"Ah, yes." Faber grimaced. "The thing that began unraveling my whole ingenious plan." He snorted. "Well, two unfortunate events came together. First, Richard was on the hiring committee when I applied for the senior professor position. He was familiar with my previous research and publication history." He rubbed a thumb over his temple. "As you are aware, the professional archaeology community is not large. At the national meetings, people had begun gossiping about Southwestern pots being sold on the black market, so to speak. Nothing anyone could put a finger on. Just vague rumors. Of course, it was my luck that after your husband had heard some these tales, one of my collectors died and his widow tried to sell his pottery." He looked at Maggie, disgusted. "You'd think the man could have handled his estate better than to just leave his collection to a wife who knew so little."

"But where does Richard come in?" Maggie was desperate to know.

"Most people would never think twice about the rumors, put two and two together. Too busy with their own professional lives, you know. But Richard. Ah, Richard. Somehow this all piqued his interest. He started by finding likely private collectors, and the thing started snowballing from there."

"But why did the collectors send their Anasazi pots to Richard? Why not keep them hidden away?" Maggie asked.

He gave her a toothy sneer, reminding her of a wolf with bared teeth. "By using an alias, I made sure every one of those collectors had plausible deniability. But they all suspected the artifacts were authentic but not legitimately salable—otherwise, why sell them in such an underhanded way? They certainly weren't going to admit it and get into trouble with the law themselves. So, when Richard asked to see particular pots, they sent them to him to maintain their image as innocent victims."

"All of them?" Maggie shook her head. "Why did Richard keep it a secret?"

Faber shifted his weight. "I thought his death—which I had nothing to do with—put an end to my nightmare of being caught, and that I was free and clear. I had the money, the pottery was hidden away in your attic, and no one was the wiser." An angry look crossed his face. "But then that special exhibition had to come up and the whole community started hunting around in their archives. I had to get those boxes before anyone else could figure out where they'd gone. Plus, I didn't know what Richard had in his notes. I couldn't risk being implicated in any way."

Maggie glared at him. His level of arrogance and dishonesty left a bitter taste in her mouth. "Was it you who nearly ran me down outside the museum after my first meeting with Linda?"

"I wasn't going to hit you. I was playing a game with you, trying to make you feel unsettled."

"You call nearly killing me a game?" Maggie scowled, clenching her hand around the flashlight.

Faber chuckled, then said, "See? Even now you're upset just thinking about it." He rubbed the top of the pile of boxes. "I'd hoped after the incident you'd want to simplify your life and not deal with the pottery. I kept offering to help, but you stubbornly refused."

Maggie stared at him. This man clearly knew no boundaries.

"And you recruited Conrad to do your dirty work. Would he have committed a crime for you? For what you told him was a higher good?"

Faber tilted his head and studied her. "What are you asking? In many ways, Conrad is a bit of a lemming. But he didn't do anything wrong."

"What about trying to throw me overboard on the boat going to South Doe Island?"

He laughed. "If I had been on that boat, I might have tried to end your increasing interference through just such an accident. I had intended to ride over with you, but when I saw Conrad on the dock, I had to abandon my plans. He thought I was out of the country. I couldn't let him see me. It would have ruined everything. And no, I don't think he had anything to do with your mishap. He doesn't have it in him. He's all bluster."

Maggie thought this over. "So, my boat escapade was an accident after all."

"And because of everything else, you had become paranoid and suspected foul play at every turn." He chuckled. "Beautiful."

His tone exuded self-satisfaction with his role in her misery over the past several days.

"I suspected Conrad because he's been so unpleasant, always suggesting that something was wrong," she said. "And that I was the cause of it."

"I wanted him to come here to pick up the pottery from you, but I didn't want him to become sociable with you in the process. Others in the department had told me about how warm and welcoming you are. I couldn't have him getting to know you. That could have put a stop to the job I wanted him to do."

Maggie kept her eyes on him, letting him brag. She wished she had her phone recording his confession, but she'd expected Eric, not this.

Faber's eyes sparkled with mischief. "My solution was brilliant, if I do say so myself. I simply told him your husband had been stealing Southwestern antiquities and that, after his death, you were continuing in the illegal marketing of First American artifacts."

Maggie's eyes widened. "You told him I was a thief?"

"Of course. He thought he was rescuing stolen goods from you. I told him I had convinced you to turn the antiquities over and that I wouldn't press charges. However, I also said I suspected you might try to keep some back or even avoid turning the stolen pots over completely. Thinking you could outsmart us, the good guys."

The whole of Faber's plan was beginning to take shape for Maggie.

"You sent those e-mails, didn't you?" she pressed on. "The ones from the department secretary."

"That was the easiest part," he said. "Our new secretary is a bit of a ditz, I'm afraid. Betsy had no respect for how important her e-mail password was. By helping her with one or two simple office computer problems, she thoughtlessly gave me her password. The rest was easy." He bestowed a Cheshire-cat grin on her. "Some people are so trusting. And so stupid."

He rubbed his hands together. "With her password and e-mail address, I was able to send letters and notes as if they came from her. And I could intercept any e-mails you sent back." He rocked his head from side to side in amusement. "Simple."

Maggie pointed to the boxes. "There are quite a few Anasazi pots from several sites. You must have been collecting them for some time."

He patted the box. "These represent years of work."

"And they all came from the collections of museums where you had done research."

"Early on in my career, I discovered that while the museums had amazing pieces of prehistoric pots and other artifacts, they never had the staff or space to properly curate them. Many were in the same containers they'd come in when donated to the museums years ago. No one had ever opened the original cartons."

"Until you showed up."

"Indeed. Given that, I realized there was little chance anyone would ever look into the containers after I'd finished my research. So when I left a museum after completing my work, I took whatever prehistoric pots I thought would bring the best price. I carefully closed and sealed their original containers and replaced them on the storage shelves. Everything looked normal." He shifted his weight. "But I had a backup plan in case someone did open a storage box. I put a note in each one saying that the materials were on loan to a museum—one that I knew had shut down because of money problems and had held an auction of their items when they closed. Most rational people would think the pots on loan had inadvertently been auctioned off. And—making everything doubly unfortunate for them—the paperwork was poor to none. It would be very difficult for anyone to trace those artifacts by the time their loss was discovered. As I thought, the museums never suspected their items were missing. It was the perfect crime."

Maggie wrinkled her brow in consternation. "I know lots of archaeologists, and none of them would do such a thing. You're supposed to be a professional. People trust you." She shook her head.

Professor Faber smirked. "Just so. That's what made this

such a success over the years. At first I was very careful, only taking one or two prehistoric artifacts. It was fun, a game. But then, I realized how easy it was to take these valuable items, as well as to sell them to collectors who would appreciate them but never let anyone know they had them." He patted the box he'd set down earlier. "I was able to slowly build a substantial nest egg. Being a professor would never allow me to enjoy the comfortable retirement I envisioned. This would."

"But then Richard discovered what you were doing, didn't he? But he didn't have any real proof. That's why he started investigating you. He never told anyone, not even me. If it turned out he was wrong and you were innocent, he didn't want to damage your reputation." Maggie practically spit the last word.

Professor Faber laughed. "Your husband was so naïve. He suspected me of robbery, but at the same time it was difficult for him to believe a fellow archaeologist would steal these remnants of America's heritage."

Faber's comments incensed Maggie. Richard was a good man who had seen the best in people. How could this despicable person, this thief, so malign her husband and what he stood for?

Faber's hand dropped behind the box and came back up with a knife. "Now that you know so much about what I've done, I'm going to have to get rid of the evidence. You."

23

Maggie stepped back while fumbling for her cell phone to call 911. Faber leaped forward, bringing the knife down toward her. Maggie frantically blocked his attack with her flashlight.

Just then, Eric burst through the front door. He tackled Professor Faber, knocking the knife out of his hand. The blade slid across the floor, landing under an armoire. Faber snatched a silver-plated candlestick from the display nearest him and struck Eric, who collapsed in a heap.

The professor stumbled. He grabbed the stair railing to steady himself. Turning toward Maggie, he raised the candlestick above his head, ready to strike.

Maggie simultaneously dialed 911 and hit the light switch, casting the room into darkness.

Faber let out a high-pitched giggle. "Ha! Now I can see you but you can't see me. Perfect."

Maggie knew her silhouette, formed by her position between him and the door, marked her location. She heard Faber move. She turned her flashlight onto strobe mode and pointed it at him.

The intense flashing lights temporarily blinded him. He dropped the candlestick and raised his arm in front of his eyes with a yell.

Maggie started for Faber. Before she took a step forward, however, another figure flew through the door. James.

Faber managed to sidestep James's attack. Arms raised against the light, the professor lurched ahead to escape through the open door. As he started past Maggie, she put her foot out and tripped him. He fell, reaching for her as he did.

She twisted away, avoiding his grasp, and swung her flashlight. It connected with his head.

James leaped on Faber to keep him down.

Sirens screamed through the night air, coming closer by the moment. Officers Clayton and Linton entered the store and ran over to where James and Faber were lying on the floor.

"There's our burglar," Maggie called out.

Officer Clayton stood with her gun ready while Officer Linton helped James up and off the professor, who lay still.

James smiled over at Maggie. "It looks like you knocked him out with your flashlight." He brushed off his pants. "So much for my theatrics."

"What you did was a lot more than theatrics," Maggie said, smiling at him. "All efforts are appreciated."

James nodded, but his eyes reflected his concern for her.

It didn't take the professor long to recover. Officer Linton pulled him to his feet. Maggie quickly filled the officers in on how she'd caught him in her shop in the act of stealing the Anasazi pottery. "And he told me plenty of interesting things."

Faber cast a swift glare at Maggie but continued to remain silent.

Officer Linton read the subdued man his rights while Officer Clayton handcuffed him. They took the professor away in the patrol car.

Once Faber was removed, Maggie, James, and Eric strolled over to Sedgwick Manor. Maggie gave Eric an ice pack for his head, then brewed coffee and pulled out the treats leftover from the morning meeting with her historical society friends. That felt like it had happened weeks ago.

Before they could settle down and discuss the night's events, however, the doorbell rang. Maggie opened the door to find Ina, looking like a miniature Sherlock Holmes in a trench coat and deerstalker hat. It was only her red tennis shoes that threw off the image.

"I heard about the break-in on my police scanner," she said, a note of excitement coloring her voice. "And that Robert and Samantha took that man to jail." She held up a brown paper bag. "I thought you might need some sustenance after such a night, so I brought you some energy bars."

Maggie laughed and invited Ina inside to join the others. As she added Ina's energy bars to the dessert plate, the others all gathered around the kitchen table. Snickers joined them and sat over by the kitchen cabinets, watching.

Ina studied Eric as she nibbled a muffin. After a moment, she leaned toward him and said in her straightforward way, "I noticed you moping around in the shop. What was that all about? You have girl troubles or something?"

Blushing a deep red, he looked down at the table, his face glum. "Yeah, I guess you could say it was something like that. I thought Connie and I had hit it off in the shop. When I saw her again on my way to the library the other day, she seemed really happy to see me." He pressed his fingers together. "Turns out I was interested in her, but it wasn't reciprocal. She already has a boyfriend." He looked up at Maggie, apologetic. "I'm sorry. I didn't realize it was so obvious. I don't think it affected my work."

"Well, I didn't notice that, particularly," Maggie said. "But I'm curious. Why were you at the shop tonight? I'm glad you were there, of course. I just didn't expect you." *Well, not after I found the professor instead, anyway.*

He beamed at her. "I've been watching the shop and your house. The first break-in at the manor bothered me a lot. I wanted to protect you and your business."

"That's why you were so tired, came in late, and even forgot your schedule," Maggie said, putting things together.

"I wasn't that good of a security guard, though." Eric hung his head. "I fell asleep in my car the night of the break-in at the shop, so I missed that one. And tonight I had to drive my dad to an appointment, so I didn't arrive at my usual time. I didn't see the guy go into the antiques shop. Doesn't help that he parked his getaway van around back. I did see you go in, though, and not come out. You didn't turn the lights on right away, and I couldn't tell what was happening. I was sure something was wrong, so I approached the building to make sure you were all right. When I got close, the lights finally went on and I saw you in a standoff. And then he moved to threaten you. I had to do something."

Ina patted his hand. "Always the protector, first in the military and now at home."

A blush rose up into Eric's cheeks, making him look more boyish.

After all her worrying, Eric's explanation was so simple and innocent. Yet there was one more thing that bothered Maggie. "Eric, I'm curious about your American archaeology class at the community college—"

Before she could finish, he interrupted. "Oh, that wasn't with the community college. They don't offer the class, not even online. It was with the University of Arizona." He continued, "You can take classes anywhere through the Internet. It's amazing."

"How true," Maggie said. She looked at James. "And why were you there?"

"I confess to being worried about you too. When you hung up the phone, I called the police to tell them you had another intruder at the shop. Then I immediately drove over to make sure you were all right." He grinned at her. "But you seemed to be doing just fine without me."

. . . .

Maggie woke up the next morning with a sense of peace. As happened often upon waking, her mind went to Richard. Since he had died so unexpectedly, she had grieved not only for his passing but also for her inability to say a final goodbye. Now, for the first time in years, she felt grief release its grip on her heart.

She realized now that she had misunderstood Richard's moodiness in the weeks before he died. She had worried it was due to a problem in their relationship. Now she knew it was this terrible burden he carried, as he unearthed Professor Faber's crime of stealing invaluable cultural artifacts and selling them. From what she could understand, if he had lived, Richard was on the verge of exposing Faber as a thief.

With the arrest of the professor—and a plan in mind to explain everything to Conrad and ask him to return all of the stolen pottery to its rightful owners—Maggie felt she'd helped her husband in his final project. It was time to move forward, unfettered by uncertainties of the past.

She glanced over at Snickers curled up in his cat bed. He looked contented, at home. She watched him for a minute, a small smile on her lips.

Throwing the covers aside, she got up to meet the new day. She slipped on jeans and a long-sleeved cotton blouse, topping it with a cardigan to keep away the spring chill. She grabbed her purse and headed out to The Busy Bean.

She had agreed to meet James for breakfast, and she didn't want to be late.

Up to this point, we've been doing all the writing. Now it's *your* turn!

Tell us what you think about this book, the characters, the bad guy, or anything else you'd like to share with us about this series. We can't wait to hear from *you!*

Log on to give us your feedback at:
https://www.surveymonkey.com/r/AntiqueShop

Annie's FICTION